Lock Down Publications and Ca$h
Presents

I0637425

The Black Diamond Cartel 3

Death of a Boss

Written By
SAYNOMORE

First Edition 2024

Printed in the United States of America

Lock Down Publications
P.O. Box 944
Stockbridge, GA 30281
www.lockdownpublications.com

Like our page on Facebook: Lock Down Publications
www.facebook.com/lockdownpublications.ldp

Stay Connected with Us!

Text **LOCKDOWN** to 22828 to stay up-to-date with new
releases, sneak peaks, contests and more…

Like our page on Facebook:
Lock Down Publications

Join Lock Down Publications/The New Era Reading Group

Visit our website:
www.lockdownpublications.com

Follow us on Instagram:
Lock Down Publications

Email Us: We want to hear from you!

Acknowledgements

First and foremost, I want to acknowledge my heavenly father and my lord and savior Christ Jesus. I want to thank them for walking me through these troubled times. I want to thank my big bro Cast from Lockdown Publication for being right here with me the whole time. I want to give a special acknowledgement to Coffee, the Queen of Lockdown Publication, may you sleep in peace in Paradise forever, love and miss. I want to thank my mother, my children, I want to thank all my readers for supporting me. I just want to say to everybody out there I greatly appreciate you, thank you for believing in me and supporting me, it means the world to me. Thanks for the awesome promotion team.

Much love,
Author Saynomore

PROLOGUE

Jasmine looked around the restaurant from the VIP seat, watching the security guards posted up by the doors. She had a 10:00 am appointment with Kevin Locke, AKA Hardbody. She looked at her watch. It was 9:55 am. She looked down at the restaurant floor and saw Kevin walking with the security guards. He stopped one of the waiters and told him something in his ear before walking off. Within 5 minutes Kevin was walking up to Jasmine. Jasmine stood up and shook his hand. Kevin smiled at her and nodded at his bodyguards, giving them a signal to walk off before he took his seat at the table with Jasmine.

"Kevin, thank you for seeing me. I greatly appreciate you taking the time out for me."

"You're welcome, Jasmine. Trust and believe me, the pleasure is all mine. So, tell me, what can I do for you?"

Jasmine licked her lips before talking and took a deep breath. "Kevin, in four words, I need a friend."

Kevin smiled when Jasmine said that and pulled out a Cuban cigar and lit it. "Jasmine, after you reached out to me, I had a background check done on you and I was very impressed with what came back."

Jasmine just looked at Kevin before speaking, taking in the words she just heard. "I stand on loyalty and I'll die a hundred times before I break my word or betray my friends. Blood makes you related but what Malachi did for us, he showed us what true loyalty meant and that's what made us family."

Kevin pulled on his Cuban cigar and nodded. "I respect everything you just said, but that does beg the question, Jasmine. Why do you need a friend? Your reputation shows you can go toe to toe with the best of them. You are a female who doesn't fear death; who doesn't have the fragrance of weakness coming off of her."

"Because I'm alone and I don't trust anybody since Malachi's murder."

"Jasmine, do you know why Malachi was killed?"

Jasmine looked into Kevin's eyes when he asked her that question.

"He was becoming too powerful. The mafia wanted him dead. They feared him. They fired one hundred shots and missed ninety-nine. The last bullet ended his life."

Before Kevin could say anything, the waiter brought them a bottle of wine and a bucket of ice with two wine glasses.

"Jasmine, is that why you think he was killed?"

"Yes. A pawn became a king and they had to stop him. They feared what they couldn't control."

Kevin poured them a glass of wine before replying to Jasmine. "Jasmine, Malachi was killed because he took a blood oath and didn't honor it. With a blood oath, you kill everyone. He left the spark alive that could have turned into a wildfire. When word got back to Mrs. Blanka, she put the spark out, then she had Malachi killed for his disloyalty. You said to me you stand on loyalty and you would die a hundred times before you broke it, so my question to you is, do you stay loyal to a man who was disloyal to a blood oath, or do you stay loyal to loyalty and respect the murder of Malachi because of his disloyalty to a blood oath?"

Jasmine was lost for words after hearing what Kevin said.

"Jasmine, think about what I just said. Are you loyal to loyalty, or are you loyal to disloyalty?"

"Kevin, how would I answer a question like that? Be loyal to loyalty or loyal to someone who was disloyal, not to me but to an oath? But who's always been loyal to me? What would you do? If that situation came to you, how would you handle it with someone that you love? How would you choose?"

"Jasmine, your followers are only as strong as their leader. Come, let me show you something."

Jasmine followed Kevin to his office to a picture hanging over the fireplace and next to the picture was a gun and a frame. Jasmine looked at the picture, and then the gun in the frame, then at the picture of Kevin standing next to the man smiling as if they were best friends. Jasmine turned around and looked at Kevin. "Who is he, Kevin?"

Kevin picked up the picture, looking at it. "His name was One Hundred. He was my best friend, my brother, the one man in the world I knew I could trust. A 31-year friendship came to an end by the gun on the wall in the frame and its shell next to the gun. It's the bullet that killed him."

"You killed him?"

Kevin put the picture back on the shelf next to the gun and a frame as a reminder what happens with disloyalty. "Yes, I killed him. Years of loyalty do not matter compared to one act of disloyalty. You asked me what would I do. Let me tell you what I did. I hugged him, kissed him on the forehead. I stepped back, then I ordered his death. He took a blood oath. It didn't honor his contract by doing that. He put the gun to his head and killed himself."

Jasmine nodded, knowing the truth now. "So, what about Nikki? What do I do with her now?"

"Let her stay in Harlem, you take Brooklyn, and if steps step out of line... In my Nino Brown voice, *rockabye baby*. Send her on a trip that she won't come back from."

Both of them started laughing.

"Jasmine, you have a friend, but understand this friendship goes both ways."

Jasmine walked up to Kevin and kissed him on the right cheek. Kevin kissed her back on her left cheek.

"You have my loyalty, Kevin."

"And you have mine, Jasmine."

Both of them took a sip out of their wine glasses to seal their bond to friendship.

Chapter 1

Nikki stepped out of the car, walking beside both of her bodyguards into the project building. Shady called her and told that they found Two Times. She'd been looking for him. When she walked to the basement, she saw Two Times and someone else tied to a chair. She looked at Shady and Cordell then back at the female. She pointed at the female with the black bag over her hair. "Who the fuck is she and why the fuck is she here?"

"Nikki, she was in the house with this nigga when we kicked the door in, so we yanked her ass up, too."

"So why the fuck did you bring her back here? You should have killed her ass and brought me Two Times. Now you got two bodies to bury, Cordell." Nikki looked back at the girl and she was shaking out of control. She could hear her cries through the duct tape covering her mouth. Nikki knew she was going to kill her but she was collateral damage. Two Times' blood was the only blood she wanted on her hands for running off with two birds like she was a bird bitch. She was going to show him she was nothing to play with. "Cordell, take the bag off of his head and duct tape off his mouth. I want to look into his eyes and hear his voice. Has he begged for his life? Two Times, I'm going to show you there ain't no ant hill too small for you to die on when you fuck with my money."

Cordell walked up to Two Times and took the bag off his head and duct tape off his mouth.

He took a deep breath then looked at Nikki before talking. "Nikki, that's my little sister. She has nothing to do with this. You want my blood. She's innocent of all of this. On God she is."

"How the fuck do you sound? She was in the house with you, right; enjoying the fruits of your labor from the shit you stole from me? So, fuck that little bitch. Matter fact, I'm going to have that hoe killed first."

"Nikki, I have your money."

"Nigga, it ain't about the money. I don't give a fuck about the money. Like I don't give a fuck about your little sister's life. You tried me like I was a straight pussy bitch. You should have known my gorillas were going to find you and bring your monkey ass back to the tree house."

"Nikki, what you want me to do with them?"

Nikki cut her eyes at Cordell and shook her head with a crooked smile. "He tried me like a bird so I'm going to treat him like a bird. Bring him to the top of the roof and throw his ass off. Let's see if he can fly."

"What about her?"

"What's the three major rules in the cartel? No gun, no witness, no bodies. Her blood is on your hands, so kill the bitch."

"Nikki, she really didn't have nothing to do with this. She's a college girl."

"Cordell, why the fuck are you questioning me? I thought you were a killer. Cordell, it's starting to be clear to me you ain't got the heart for this shit no more. I'm smelling fragrances of weakness on you. If you can't kill that bitch, I'll kill her." Nikki walked up to Cordell until she was face to face with him and looked him in the eyes. "Then I'm going to kill you, if you can't get your head in the game. We are apex predators. I don't give a fuck about an innocent life. Now kill this bitch and throw this pussy ass nigga off the roof." Nikki looked at both of them, turned around and walked off with her bodyguards as Cordell walked up to the girl in the chair with his gun out. All Nikki heard was the gunshot as she was walking out of the basement.

***

Jasmine walked into the penthouse.

Kareem looked at her. "Jasmine where were you at?" He stood by the window smoking a cigar.

"Kareem, did you ever ask yourself who had enough heart to kill Malachi? Do you know why Malachi was killed?"

"Malachi had a price on his head and karma came back and collected on it. It's the fucking life we live, Jasmine. Live today, die tomorrow. Everybody can't win in this game, and when that nigga bodied Malachi, he won the game. He hit the buzzer, but you still didn't tell me where you were at."

"I went to make a friend, and I know why Malachi was killed."

Kareem walked up to Jasmine and said in aggressive voice, "Who the fuck is your friend and what do you mean you know why Malachi was killed? Jasmine, you need to start spilling the beans on this conversation you had with your so-called friend."

"Hardbody is a new friend in the cartel. Mrs. Blanka had Malachi killed."

Kareem pulled from his cigar. "Because Hardbody told you this you believe it?"

"Kareem, we laid the murder game down. We bodied niggas left and right. We didn't give a fuck who you were; our bullets never had no names on them. We just made a point to all— even them noodle-eating, pizza-loving fat fucks, even the crackers who gave Malachi Brooklyn, we bodied. Malachi got killed because he didn't honor his blood oath to the cartel. The cartel killed him. He was disloyal and I ain't pulling nobody off the block for a nigga who couldn't honor his word. Malachi's death was yesterday and I'm thinking about today."

"Do you hear yourself, Jasmine? The same nigga that always had your back; you saying fuck him because he's in a box."

"Yeah, I do, Kareem. I know what I'm saying. I ain't worried about a fucking man that's dead. I'm thinking about me and your future and what's ahead of us right now."

Kareem smiled as he relit his cigar, shaking his head, looking at Jasmine. "I don't give a fuck if Malachi broke a hundred blood oaths. That was my fucking brother and I can't wait to put that bitch Mrs. Blanka in a cold fucking grave."

"Then you are putting a gun to your own fucking head as well, Kareem."

"Then I'm playing Russian roulette and I'm going to see how many times I can pull the trigger before that bitch goes off." Kareem looked at Jasmine one more time before walking out of the penthouse slamming the door behind him.

Jasmine already knew there was going to be blood in the streets and she was ready for a new body count.

Chapter 2

Private Investigator Oldham sat at his desk looking over pictures and videos of Nikki Gunz and her crew along with the victims they left behind. She was deadlier than anybody he ever came across. He no longer worked for the police department, he was a private investigator and he only took the cases he wanted. Ever since his kidnapping and the threats to his family he kept his eyes on Malachi and his crew. All the intel he had was for his personal records and he never let anybody else see them.

There was a folder on his desk with pictures inside... some things you can't forget, some things you can't take back, and some things you wish you never got involved in. Or at least that's what he said to himself every time he looked at that file knowing the pictures that were inside were a blessing and a curse, along with a death wish all in one. Although, it could be a blessing for the right price. He defined it as a curse because he had a death wish if it ever got out there he had them.

He pulled on his cigarette and opened the file and was looking at the pictures he took two years ago of new cartel boss, Nikki Gunz and Mrs. Blanka, head over the deadliest cartel in Mexico talking to Malachi Williams as Nikki Gunz had her gun pointed at his head. That night he witnessed the execution of Malachi Williams and the rise of Nikki Gunz becoming the new head of the Black Diamond Cartel. The friendship of Nikki Gunz and Miss Blanka was solidified that night as Nikki kissed her hand and cheek as a sign of respect. He was lost for words watching Malachi Williams, the untouchable don take multiple shots and Nikki Gunz standing over the top of his dead body still shooting him. 2 years later that night still haunted him and he wished that he never followed Nikki Gunz that night, but like he said to himself, some shit you just can't take back.

Nikki Gunz became too powerful in Harlem as well in the five boroughs. Oldham lost his thoughts when he saw the brief newscast about a man being thrown off a building in Harlem and a female shot in the head laying next to his dead body. He knew this was the work of Nikki Gunz and this was going to be a cold case because no one was going to speak against her. He put his cigarette out and walked out his office to go see a old friend. A body in the streets of Harlem was normal when Nikki had her apes and Harlem was her jungle.

***

"Roulette, you and Remy post up over here. This is your block and your building, this is where Nikki wants you and this is how you are going to get your respect out here. How we talk is our murder game, niggas only respect violence and we don't get ate by the niggas in the streets. Harlem is our jungle and we are the apes who run it… we beat on our chest and live by the oath of shoot or get shot. And always, always keep a round in the chamber, guns ready to blaze."

"We got you Shady." Shady nodded at Roulette when she said that.

"Copy that, then I'm going to let the niggas in the spot know y'all out front on the block." Shady walked off, closing doors behind him.

"Remy, we are on the block now…mixing it up with the killers and gorillas."

14

"Roulette, let's let these niggas know who the fuck we are...Remy Kartel and Roulette Stone, the two deadliest bitches in the Blood Diamond Cartel."

"Fucking right, Remy." Remy looked at the black Hummer pulling up, Roulette and Remy both had their hands on their guns as the Hummer came to a stop in front of their building, when the door opened up Kareem stepped out looking at them not staying a word.

"Y'all must be the two new apes on the block." Remy cut her eyes at Kareem and grilled him.

"Yo, I don't know who the fuck you are my guy, do you have business here? Because if not you need to step back in your Hummer and pull the fuck off."

"Little girl, if you know who the fuck I am you would know I will pull your tongue out your mouth and make you eat that bitch." Before Remy could say something Shady walked up to Kareem with his gun in his hand til he was in his face.

"Nigga you must be lost." Kareem smiled as he looked at Shady with his gun in his hand.

"Nigga you must have forgot I was the man who brought you into this game when you were just a little nigga in the park selling 20 sacks of dope that you stole from the nigga who was fucking your moms."

"You're a funny nigga, but I'm older now and you are an ops so you could do what Remy Kartel said get back in your Hummer and pull off, or I can see if that Versace shirt you have on is bulletproof and that's the only fucking warning I'll give because I know you nigga."

"Nikki really got you and Cordell gassed up... y'all be safe out here, these streets are dangerous niggas get bodied everyday."

"Yeah, take note to that nigga... because next time you pull up on this block we ain't talking on the diamond, we blazing."

"Alright my nigga, keep that same energy facts." Kareem got back in the Hummer and looked at Shady as he put up his middle finger at all of them as he drove off. Shady turned around and looked at Remy and Roulette with his gun in his hand.

"Next time that fool shows his face on this block pop his top, he just got added to the grocery list." Roulette and Remy nodded as Shady walked off to his black on black BMW parked in front of the building.

Chapter 3

Nikki walked out the diner talking to Cali as she sipped on her morning coffee.

"Nikki, I don't know how true the story is… but word is that Jasmine made a new friend." Nikki smiled as she looked at Cali.

"And who is this new friend?"

"Hard Body, from Queens."

"Hard Body? He knows Bop."

"You're right, but he's one of them cowboy ass niggas…live by the gun die by the gun, that Billy the Kid level shit."

"And Billy the Kid died by the gun, so I hope Hard Body knows his history because we can make history repeat itself."

"Let's just hope we don't have to, Nikki. You already have a high body count and the police are already investigating us, just because we don't see them doesn't mean anything."

"I'm not worried about the cops, I have cops on my payroll. I got this Cali, now come on… I have a meeting with Mrs. Blanka and I don't want to be late." Nikki's driver looked to the left as he opened the door for her to get inside and that's when he saw a black van coming their way with the sliding door open and two masked men who were pointing Mac 11s at them. He jumped in front of Nikki and pulled his gun out.

Nikki dropped her cup of coffee on the ground as her driver jumped in front of her pulling his gun out as he started to shoot at the van. All you heard were the sound of gunshots going off. Nikki ducked down behind her driver as blood sprayed all over her as the van peeled off. Her driver dropped down to his knees as he let his guns drop in front of him to the ground. He turned around and looked at Nikki with blood trailing out of his mouth. his body slumped backwards on the ground and Nikki looked at all the blood on his shirt from the multiple shots he took to the chest protecting her.

Nikki crawled over to him and was lifting up his head as bubbles of blood were coming out of his mouth. Suddenly, people started coming out the diner watching everything unfold. Nikki took her hand and wiped the blood from his mouth as she held his hand as he took his last breath.

Nikki had tears in her eyes as she looked Dead in his eyes as the sound of the police sirens were getting closer. She stood up when the police car stopped in front of the scene, two blue and white officers walked up to her, assessing the scene the officers looked at the body and then her with blood all over her shirt.

"Miss, can you tell me what happened out here?" Nikki looked the officer in the face.

"I don't remember anything, it all happened so fast… within a blink of an eye." That's when Detective Keith Waters walked up to them with a bottle of water in his hand, he looked at Nicki then the officers.

"You two, go tape this crime scene off. I don't need nobody messing up the crime scene."after the two offices walked off, Detective Waters took a sip of his water and guided Nikki away from the body where nobody could hear them.

"Nikki, I don't know what happened out here but I know that's your driver. Do I need to remind you we don't need bodies dropping right now. It's hot, let things cool down… especially after the body was thrown off the roof in Harlem and a college girl with a bullet in the head. Harlem is super hot right now."

"You've got to be fucking kidding me? Motherfuckers just tried to take me out. I don't give a fuck that Harlem is on fire, this bitch is about to go up in flames blazing. You're down here talking about a body count, are you fucking kidding me? You know what the fuck you need to worry about is getting a good supply of body bags, because my shooters don't miss. This nigga came after me, proof of kill is a head shot. What the fuck do I pay you to do? Clean this shit up, we're done here." Detective Keith Waters looked at Nikki as she walked off.

Chapter 4

"What the fuck you mean you missed? So let me get this right, she comes out the diner with her driver... you watch her from the van parked a few cars down, y'all have the drop on her with not one, but two shooters. Let's not forget the two Mac 11s, basically y'all are at point blank range from this bitch and you fucking miss? How? Can someone please tell me how the fuck do you mess that up?"

"Boss, her driver never ran... he stood in front of her using his body as a shield shooting right back at us." Hardbody turned around and looked at them.

"I don't want anybody to know we were the ones that took the shot. Nikki let the streets talk so let's hear what they have to say. Where's the van at now?"

"Burnt under the bridge in Brooklyn?"

"I'm going to say this once and only once because I don't like having the same conversation twice. Next time I send you to kill a motherfucker, get the job done. I don't care if you have to jump out of the fucking van and kill everyone around you, don't never come back to me with a sad story again. Do I make myself clear?"

"Yeah boss?" both of them said.

"Good, now the both of y'all leave me."

***

Kareem lowered his head as he lit his cigar before talking to Jasmine.

"Jasmine, I don't know, but them hitters you have on the streets you might need to pull them off the block. Shit just got real."

"Kareem, what are you talking about?"

"Word just got back to me that your new friend Hardbody just popped the bottle on Nikki and his shot missed." Kareem said in a smooth low tone to Jasmine.

"How do you know it was Hardbody who sent his shooters after Nikki?"

"Because Hardbody is old school, two shooters and a black van shooting up one of her spots. Everybody knows he's a cowboy, he flipped the coin made the play and fumbled the ball."Jasmine took her phone out as she walked off and dialed the number, a few seconds later Hardbody answered the phone.

"Jasmine,"

"Why didn't you tell me you were going to send a hundred shots at Nikki? Your guys missed and now she's going to come back 10 times harder. I know this bitch, I know how she moves, I know how she thinks." Kareem walked up behind Jasmine as he smoked his cigar listening to her conversation.

"Fuck that bitch, that was just a warning shot. The next shots her driver won't be the only one getting bodied, that was just to let that hoe know to stay in her place."

"Just be on point because she's coming back with the hand of God and they ain't the type of bitch to simply roll over."

"Then she'll be the type of bitch to die."

"Just be ready because when it rains it pours."Jasmine hung up the phone and looked at Kareem as he pulled onto his cigar looking at her intently.

"So what you have to say now Kareem?"

"Guns up, because the storm is coming and Shady and Cordell both know how we move."

"Guns up then, let's make these niggas bleed." Jasmine said before she walked off.

***

Nikki sat perched at the edge of her desk smoking a cigar as she looked at her apes in the office. She never changed her clothes, they still had Cali's blood on them. Roulette and Remy stood behind everyone else as they looked at Nikki, nobody said a word. They always waited for Nikki to talk, she looked at Roulette as she put her cigar down in the ashtray.

"Hardbody wanted me dead today, but here I stand in front of all of y'all. His shooters missed, I don't give a fuck about killing a nigga as everybody here knows. I'll hold the 45 myself and hop out of the car and shoot that bitch myself. Motherfuckers think shit is sweet with us, or that he's the untouchable. Fuck nigga just don't know we coming out swinging, we don't lay the fuck down. I guess that was his warning shot, but when the fuck has it been cool to get shot at and not shoot back. This nigga came to the jungle shooting at me, so since he wanted to play in the woods, he's going to be in the woods for good. I want you to put so much pressure on this nigga I don't even want him to fall asleep comfortable. I don't want him to feel comfortable in his skin, this motherfucker just try to pull rank on me but this shit he tried today we're going to show him he won't win. I want this motherfucker laid up stiff, his shooters missed but the motherfuckers I'm sending ain't going to miss. Y'all want to put a smile on my face, body that nigga. As in put a ribbon on him for me, I want to turn on the news and see on Channel 5 that nigga went to hell. I don't give a fuck if the police are around they better get ready for the shootout of the century. You better beat on your fucking chest because we're here now, we got the streets on lock. When we're done the mayor is going to go "Whoa now, let's handle this like grownups," we clear?" Nicki looked around and nodded she already knew the streets were about to be running red but her shooters don't miss. *Game on,* she thought to herself.

Chapter 5

Every officer and detective was in the briefing room as the lead investigator walked into the room and up to the blackboard and pointed at pictures of Nikki Gunz.

"Nikki Gunz's driver was gunned down in front of her diner 3 days ago. There are three major players in New York, the Italians have not been on the scene in the last few years the only ones that are making any noise is Nikki Gunz and her apes as she calls them in Harlem. In addition you have Jasmine and Kareem in Brooklyn since Malachi Williams' murder they've been keeping low key, and then you have Kevin Mosley, AKA Hardbody— he's been running the Bronx and Queens for years now. Our intel tells us that Jasmine had a private meeting with Kevin Mosley last week and guess what… they became friends. The same source told us that Hardbody was the one who sent his shooters at Nikki Gunz 3 days ago when her driver was killed. Ladies and gentlemen, there's a shit storm coming our way it's coming straight to New York, and if we don't stop it A a of people are going to die. What I can tell you about Nikki Gunz, Hardbody, Kareem, and Jasmine, is killing a motherfucker is as easy as cutting the lights off in their house, they do it everyday it doesn't bother them."

"Do you want us to put two teams out there on round the clock surveillance watching all the suspects ma'am?"

"No, it would be a waste of manhours and taxpayers dollars. Any one of them could pick up the phone and make a call and get the job done."

"Detective Keith, put everyone on the streets. We need to let them know that we control the streets, history shows us they are not scared to kill a cop, so keep your eyes open. If it doesn't look right, call it in and protect yourself, do not be a super cop... wait for backup. Do I make myself clear? If so meeting's adjourned."

***

The black limo pulled up to the docks and Nikki waited for her door to open. Once it did she stepped outside the limo and looked around at all the bodyguards that Mrs. Blanka had standing around holding assault riffles. She and Cordell walked up on the yacht together, once they reached the door both of them got patted down and their guns were removed by the bodyguard he stepped aside and let Nikki into the room but stopped Cordell from entering. Nikki looked at him and nodded let him know to wait there as she turned around and walked inside. Mrs. Blanka sat at the table having a drink when Nikki walked in she turned and looked at her as she stood and walked over to her and embraced her warmly.

"Nikki, please have a seat, there's so much we need to talk about. How have you been?"

"I want to apologize for missing our last meeting the circumstances were out of my hands."

"Darling I know everything, I heard about what happened that's why I need to talk to you." Nikki just looked at her when she said that.

"I'm confused, what's going on?"

"By now I know you know that it was Hardbody that took the shot at you and missed."

"Yeah I am aware it was him, and I plan on chopping his fucking head off... but this doesn't have anything to do with you?"

"It actually has a lot to do with me and I don't need you striking back at him, just give him this pass and let it be like a gift for him and the next time he'll die."Nikki looked at Mrs. Blanka as if she was crazy.

"His bullets killed my driver and almost killed me."

"Nikki, how many people have you killed with your bullets? Brothers, fathers, sons, daughters, your driver was killed but he knew the rules to the game... he knew what he signed up for."

"And what about loyalty? My loyalty to him, his loyalty to me cost him his life, he stood in front of them bullets that were meant for me and died to save my life. So what about my loyalty to him?"

"I'm standing on my loyalty that's why I'm here today, Jasmine saved my life many years ago if it wasn't for her I would be dead today."

"So you're telling me because of your loyalty to Jasmine, I have to be disloyal to you and to Cali?" Mrs. Blanka picked up her drink and took a sip before talking.

."Nikki, some situations are harder to walk away from than others... walk away Nikki, it would be the best for everyone."

"Mrs. Blanka if I didn't know any better I would think you just threatened me?"

"No! that's not a threat Nikki?" Nikki nodded her head.

"So then what was it then, if it wasn't a threat?"

"Let me say this to you! if you lose me as a friend that doesn't mean you would gain me as an enemy. I still want to see you eat, just not at the table with me."

"And let me say this to you, I will remain loyal to all my apes dead or alive... they took oaths to me and the Blood Diamond Cartel."

"So I guess this was a waste of time coming up here, clear your mind is already made up."

"My mind was made up 3 days ago and I would personally pull the trigger and watch her die."

"So we have nothing else to talk about then."

"I guess not,"Mrs. Blanka stood up and waved her guards in the room. Nikki got up and looked at her and walked past the guards. Once she was out the door she was handed back her gun, Cordell took his and walked behind her to the limo.

"Nikki, is everything good with Mrs. Blanka?"Nicki looked at Cordell.

"No, this is shaping up to be a bloody summer and we are about to be the underdogs, but just like the runt, the underdogs always come out on top."

"She wants you to stand down doesn't she?"

"I don't give a fuck what she wants or who's around Hardbody, when y'all see him Cali isn't going to die in vain, dead or alive we ride for ours."

"You know he stay close to his bodyguards 24 hours a day, plus a whole lot of police he has on the payroll in downtown Brooklyn and Queens."Nikki looked at Cordell as he opened the limo door for her before she stepped inside.

"I don't give a fuck if the president or the governor was down there and Hardbody was surrounded by the FBI. Y'all motherfuckers better crash out and anybody around that motherfucker better get ready for a shootout of the century, you understand?" Cordell didn't say anything else as Nikki got in the limo he knew her word was law.

Chapter 6

Kareem looked around... Jasmine had pulled all the hitters off the streets, they all knew who Kareem was but never seen him face to face. This was the first time they ever laid eyes on him he pulled on his cigar and looked at Jasmine before talking to them.

"A war is coming our way, Nikki has her apes running around Harlem lawlessly...that bitch doesn't have a heart. The stories y'all heard are real, her body count is real, but I don't give a fuck about no bitch in Harlem and no dirty ass monkeys beating on their collective chests. Harlem isn't even no fucking borough. So fuck Harlem, fuck Nikki, and fuck her apes. This is Brooklyn lions, tigers, and bears. BK is the real fucking jungle, we are the real killers. That bitch might have enough heart to send her apes swinging on trees down here, but if they come to the jungle they going to die in these fucking woods. I want everyone on point because shit is about to go boom, I want every ape laying under a branch fucking dead. Everybody group up in threes, no less than two at all times on the block." Jasmine walked over to Kareem and looked at everyone they all respected her as a boss bitch.

"Doesn't shit change, we are still on the block 24/7 making this money. I still want eyes on all my clubs— 4 Tray, you and Youngin, I want y'all making rounds every hour checking on everyone I know. I don't like this bitch but I respect her, once upon a time she was my sister not by choice but by the cartel, y'all be on point because like Kareem said, that bitch is coming one of hers got killed and she wants blood, and when she comes to Brooklyn that bitch is dead. That bitch's body is going to stay in Brooklyn." nobody said a word. Jasmine looked at Kareem he nodded at the door and everybody walked out the office, Kareem look back at Jasmine.

"You said this to me and this is a fact, we went up against the mob niggas in New Jersey, you and Malachi went to Mexico and killed motherfuckers in the cartel, if I know Nikki she's going to go after Hardbody. This is what I'm thinking, we put eyes on Hardbody and when her hitters pop on him, we send ours to eat on her... she won't see it coming."

"So let's toe tag this bitch."

"And what about Shady and Cordell?"

"Fuck them! they are the ops...they on the menu too."

"Fuck it then, let's treat them like some pits and get their ears and tails cut, it's time to jump out the truck with the Big Mac."

***

Drama sat on the hood of the car smoking a blunt when Mayhem walked up to him, he dapped him up then passed him the blunt.

"Drama, you ready for this shit tonight?"

"Yeah, Nikki's mind is made up, she ain't with the chit chat tonight. We are strapping up like the mob and stepping like the cartel and this nigga lost his fucking marbles. How the fuck Hardbody beefing with Nikki and haven't move his moms, his aunt, his wife, because tonight someone's going to go to the promised land."

"Real talk Drama, them nights in the trenches turned Nikki into a monster and tonight class is in session and where we taking niggas they ain't coming back from."

"I already know Mayhem, ding dong round one Nikki strikes back"

"Drama, it's time we show these niggas they be capping, pulling tricks out their hats, it's time to clap him and his followers." Drama smiled and got off the hood of his car and walked into the spot with Mayhem.

Chapter 7

Detective Oldham watched Nikki as she walked down 125th Street and Harlem with Cordell and two more bodyguards walking behind them, he followed her from Lenox Avenue to Park Avenue, all the way from the East 102nd Street. He'd been following them since 9:00 a.m. he heard about the attempt on her life and he knew she was going to strike back sooner rather than later. Stepping in front of a deli both of her bodyguards walked inside while she stood outside with Cordell, a few seconds later they came out and stood next to her as Cordell walked inside, when he came out Nikki then made her way inside as they watched the door. Nikki walked to the back table and sat down in front of Roger.

"Mac, you said you wanted to see me so tell me what can I do for you?" Mac pulled out a folder and placed it on the table.

"You are being watched Nikki, the NYPD have been watching you... they are waiting for you to strike back. They know that you are not going to let this blow over." Nikki opened the file and looked inside at all the pictures of her and Kareem, along with Jasmine and Hardbody she closed the file and looked at Mac.

"Who's running this investigation?" Mac took a deep breath before talking.

"Captain Fuller and FBI Agent Dawn, they are on your case, they want a conviction and they want you Nikki." Nikki shook her head and smiled.

"I think it's time me and Captain Fuller have a one-on-one."

"Yeah… there's one more thing you should know about."

"What is that?"

"Come let me show you?"Nikki got up and walked to the window with Mac?

"You see that gray car to the right, four cars down?"

"Yeah I do?"

"He's been following you for the last week! his name is Oldham he was a detective a few years back, but Malachi had him and his partner kidnapped. His partner was killed so he left the force and now he's a private eye."

"Some people just don't understand when you play with fire you get burned. Thank you Mac, as always your drop off will be where it always is, and one more thing, go have a meeting or talk with this Oldham."

"I will, thank you Nikki." Nikki patted Mac on the back as she walked out of the deli. Oldham watched her as she walked down to her Maybach and got inside with Cordell.

"Is everything good?"

"No, you and Shady are going to pay a visit to someone tonight… and I may just tag along with y'all, no we should do it another night, matter of fact."

"Sayless."Nikki didn't say another word as she looked out the window in the deep thought.

***

Drama looked at Mayhem and everyone else standing around them with their black hoodies on and murder one masks over their faces, guns in their hands. There were 10 of them all together

"Yo, this motherfucker violated the rules, so now they are in the mix. Tonight we are taking it to the max. I don't give a fuck if the police are waiting out there... we are crashing out tonight. We are letting them know we are the fucking problem. Nikki said the niggas she's sending aren't going to miss us, we're letting niggas know shit is real. The work we put in tonight, be proud of it niggas, we apes but we moving like the mob. After tonight this shit ain't over, we're just getting it started. We're going to show them who we are, so when they see them guns they are going to realize that they have only seconds remaining. Come on, beat on your chest... it's time we ride out." everyone looked at Drams as they cocked their guns and loaded up in the cars and vans.

***

Hardbody sat at the back table in the VIP section of the club smoking a Black and Mild, drinking a glass of gin as his bodyguards walked around the club clearing it out. It was 1:00 a.m. and there were two guys standing at the front entrance watching the club floor as Hardbody told them to as the other bodyguards cleared the floor. Hardbody stood up from the VIP section as he put his Black and Mild out and took his last shot of gin. That's when all you heard was gunshots going off. Hardbody pulled his gun out as his guards did the same, one of his guys went to turn the corner when he got shot twice, dropping him and his gun to the floor. Hardbody started shooting at the entrance as his bodyguards ran to him shooting in the same direction. Hardbody yelled to his guard,

"Get to the back door, they have the front doors covered... the car's in the back." when the guard opened the back door and went to run out to the car, Drama called him.

"Yo buddy," the guard turned around and looked at Drama as he pointed the MP at him. The guard just closed his eyes and shook his head as the rounds from Drama's gun ripped through his chest, taking his life. Hardbody heard the shots and looked at the back door as Drama was walking in, gun pointed directly at him. He looked at the front door and saw a man walking up to him with a few guys behind him, Hardbody smiled and threw his gun on the floor, he reached into his pocket and pulled out a Black and Mild and lit it before talking.

"When you kill me don't shoot me in the face, let me have an open casket so everybody can see what a real fucking boss looks like after death." Drama walked up to him and put his gun to his face.

"Pussy nigga, you living right now because we ain't going to kill you... this shit is personal."

"So who the fuck is going to do it then? Where the fuck they at? You want me to beg for my life... I'm a real boss, my name is Hardbody." Hardbody looked around at everybody and that's when he looked at the front door and saw Nikki walking in with 2 in red bottom shoes, blue skin-tight jeans with ribs in them, a red Polo shirt, topped with a blue Pelle Pelle coat. Her hair was pulled back in a ponytail and a gun in her hand. Cordell and Shady walking right beside her as she walked up to Hardbody until they were face to face.

"I see you put two and two together, killing me ain't going to stop anything, do you know who the fuck is backing me?"

"Hardbody! I had a talk already with Mrs. Blanka you think I give a fuck if she's backing you? You don't understand that it's the Blood Diamond Cartel, I don't give a fuck about nothing else. You killed my friend, you killed my ape, now I'm looking at a dead man in the eyes." Hardbody pulled on his Black and Mild and smiled.

"Nikki, you think what you did was honor... you think you are trained like the cartel. I know your secret Nikki, but I ain't no rat... so it's coming to the grave with me. " Cordell looked at Shady when he heard that, Nikki put her gun to Hardbody's face.

"Honor that, pussy." the sound of the gun echoed through the club as Hardbody fell backwards on the floor. Nikki walked up to him and shot him three more times in the chest and then she looked at her apes as she made her point.

"Let's get the fuck out of here, now." she said as she walked off. Cordell looked at Shady and then at Hardbody's corpse laying in a pool of blood before he followed Nikki out of the club thinking about what Hardbody said before she killed him.

Chapter 8

It was 8:00 a.m. when Chief Ward and Captain Fuller walked into Hardbody's nightclub and looked around the crime scene, they walked up to Detective Keith.

"Detective Keith, what happened down here last night?"

"If I had to guess the shootout of the century, Captain Fuller. We have seven bodies, all Hardbody's men. The four under the white sheet out front, the one over there by the back door, and the one by the front door. We have Kevin Locke, AKA Hardbody, under this sheet over there by the VIP, and one more outback. Now the picture I'm seeing is Nikki's crew came in shooting it out and at the front of the club they bodied these guys, made their way inside, the one over there— Hardbody's guard ran out the back door to the car, but Nikki had someone already out there, they killed him and then they took out Hardbody last."

"Who was on this beat last night?"

"I don't know sir, but I'll find out."

"Good, give me a full report on my desk, Detective." Captain Fuller and Chief Ward walked away from Detective Keith's hearing.

"Captain Fuller, get ready for a body count unlike any you've seen. The storm is here and we are in the middle of the eye." Captain Fuller didn't say anything because he knew that was the truth.

***

Kareem was on the deck smoking a cigar looking over the city of New York when Jasmine walked out there. When he caught sight of the look on her face he knew something was wrong with her.

"What do you need to tell me Jasmine?"

"Last night Hardbody and his men was killed."

"I told you that nigga was a bum, his time's been up... he just had a line of respect, but a bitch like Nikki? She doesn't give a fuck about who you used to be, she's a show me type of bitch."

"So let's show this bitch who we are." Kareem shook his hand.

"Yeah, let's show her, she thinks she's the untouchable but she's not. It's time to show her that, who reached out to you about her body?"

"Nobody, it was on the news."

"Let them niggas know to watch who they drink with and who they smoke with, we don't need Nikki getting the drop on us because when we pop up it's going to be Nikki's last prayer. It's going to be the second she breathes her last breath of air." Jasmine nodded and walked off.

***

Mrs. Blanka sat on her deck sipping a glass of wine and eating out of a fruit basket when her sliding glass door opened and her driver Rico was standing there. She smiled at him and waved for him to come out and join her on the deck.

"Rico, come have a seat with me out here and tell me the news you have for me." Rico closed the glass doors and sat at the table with Mrs. Blanka.

"Now, tell me Rico what do you have?"

37

"Nikki, from the Blood Diamond Cartel killed Hardbody and a few of his men the other night." Mrs. Blanka took a sip of her wine.

"I knew that was going to happen, the look in her eyes told me everything I needed to know from the last conversation I had with her."

"So, where do we go from here?"

"She's dead to us, I gave her two options: Option A— she walks away and takes the loss, or Option B— we walk away from her. She chose Option B so we have no more ties with Nikki, she is cut off from everything."

"With the utmost respect, Mrs. Blanka anybody else that went against your word you would have killed, why is she getting the pass?"

"Because she did what Malachi couldn't do, he left Cruise alive. When I talked to Nikki she came down here dressed up like a call girl and cut Cruise's neck from ear to ear, not only did she kill him... she also brought me back Cruise's heart. That's the only reason she has the pass with me, and she only gets one, the next time her heart will be the one that's brought back to me." Rico got up from the table leaving Mrs. Blanka to her own thoughts, she sat and thought about the first lesson she told Nikki, that was the hardest choice required the strongest will and Nikki's will was unbreakable.

Chapter 9

Mayhem sat in a cut, smoking a Newport outside of the auto parts shop behind the dumpster when Cordell came walking up, smoking a blunt talking over the phone. He was so deep in his conversation he didn't see Mayhem as he was talking, Mayhem heard him say Nikki's name so he pulled his phone out and started recording him

"Look Karo, I know we went our own way but I swear to God she looked Hardbody in the eyes when Hardbody said your secret is safe with me, I'm taking it to the grave with me. He looked Nikki in the eye before she pulled the trigger, she said honor them and then she flatlined him. Son, look fuck the last few years Kareem, this is bigger than me and you, this is about Malachi. I think Nikki killed him dead." Mayhem didn't say a word, he just watched him before he seen Cordell flick the blunt on the ground as he said, "Cool, I'll be there tonight bro," then he walked away. Once he said that Mayhem walked the other way out of sight knowing that Cordell just fucked up.

***

Captain Fuller pulled up at his house and stepped out of the car, he stretched and yawned he looked at his watch and noticed it was 10:00 p.m. He walked to his front door and put the key inside as he unlocked the door he walked inside.

39

He stopped when he stepped in something wet, he turned the lights on and spotted a pool of blood on the floor.

"What the fuck?" was all Captain Fuller could say as he looked at the thick pool of blood, that's when Drama came from around the corner pointing a black 9 Miller at his head. Drama saw when he had his hand ready, he went to reach for his gun on his waist.

"Try me fucking gangster, the last sound you're going to hear is a boom." Captain Fuller shook his head and that's when he heard a gun cocked behind him, he saw Shady pointing a gun at his face.

"Captain Fuller, this can go two ways... you can either take a ride with us or you could go see your watch dog face to face. If you wonder whose blood is all over the floor, I don't have time to be fighting with no fucking dog at all, so are you taking a ride or are you just going to die right here tonight?"

"How do I know where you're taking me, or that there's not a gun there with a bullet with my name on it waiting for me?"

"If a nigga wanted you dead, you'll be dead. Someone just wants to have a word with you." Captain Fuller nodded.

"Yeah, come on let's go." Shady took the gun from his waist and the one that he had on his ankle, he knew he had them covered. They walked outside to the black Hummer and put him inside, Captain Fuller knew Nikki was the one who wanted to see him.

***

Cordell walked up to the back of the warehouse where he saw Kareem and Jasmine standing next to Jasmine's Benz. Kareem was smoking a cigar as Cordell walked up to him.

"Jasmine is here because whatever you have to say about Malachi she needs to hear, like you said this is bigger than me and you, it's about Malachi."

"Jasmine."

"Cordell, so what do you have to tell us about Malachi? I already know that Mrs. Blanka had him killed for not honoring his blood oath." Cordell took a deep breath.

"I think Nikki was the one that killed him, or she had him killed... even if it was Mrs. Blanka who gave the order, she still went against the family." Jasmine pointed her finger at Kareem when Cordell said that.

"I fucking told you that bitch had her hands in Malachi's murder."

"Why the fuck you say that? Cordell! where the fuck is this shit coming from?"

"As I told you over the phone, Hardbody told Nikki that he knew her secret, you think what you did was honor?"

"You know what Kareem? I don't know if she did it or not, but we need to hurry up and kill this bitch. Cordell, I don't fuck with you, you went to work for the bitch and you went against us you are a fucking traitor." Kareem looked at Cordell

"How can we get her? What is her weakness, what is her weak link?"

"She don't have a weak link... that bitch's heart is cold. She's too smart she's been around the Medellin Cartel, with Escobar's sons talking face to face. She's becoming one of the most powerful and violent drug cartels in New York and Harlem. Nick is responsible for a major share of the cocaine, she's becoming known for her ruthlessness, committed for the crazy acts of violence. She doesn't give a fuck about kidnapping and murder, and she's about to become more powerful in a few more weeks. She has a meeting with the Louisiana Sicilian Mafia" Jasmine shook her head.

"She's having a meeting with the *Costa Nostra?* They don't even deal with black people, but they want to have a meeting with her."

"Cordell, find her weak link so we can body this bitch before we become the ones in the black bags."

Cordell nodded and dapped Kareem up, he looked at Jasmine.

"Look, I just told you we ain't cool… you still work for that bitch, you are an ape." Jasmine sucked her teeth then walked to the car. Kareem just shook his head and turned around and walked off.

***

The black Hummer stopped on the deck, Shady opened the door for Captain Fuller to get out. Drama walked up to Captain Fuller and looked him dead in the eyes, Captain Fuller looked at the night air past Drama before looking at him.

"So where is Nikki Gunz at?"

"You are about to see her, and y'all two are about to have a one-on-one talk. Let me tell you now though, you might come get me for kidnapping, you and I might even get locked up but if you touch Nikki I promise you this, I'll be the last thing you see before you talk to God. Now come on, she's waiting for you." Captain Fuller walked onto the boat and was told to walk down the stairs when he walked in the room Nikki was sitting down in a chair smoking a cigar, Drama escorted Captain Fuller to his seat.

"Captain, have a seat and remember what I said to you." Nicki looked at Drama and nodded. Drama walked out the room and closed the door behind him, Captain Fuller felt the boat pulling away from the docks as Nikki placed her cigar down in the ashtray.

"I hope you don't mind the cigar, Malachi got me smoking them… after the first one you are hooked or not on them."

"I don't mind the smoke, but where are you taking me if you don't mind me asking?"

"Just for a little ride, Captain."

"Stacy, what happened to you? This isn't you."

"Captain, do you know what happened to me after we did the interview on Wake up New York?"

"No, I don't." Captain Fuller said in a low tone.

"You want to know what happened to me? I was raped, branded, forced to sell drugs, and kill innocent people. My family was threatened... do you know how it feels to do what you were told by force? Stacy Hall is dead, and Nikki Gunz is alive now." Captain Fuller was lost for words.

"So what really happened to Malachi? How did he get killed?'

"He got himself killed by having a weak heart. Captain Fuller, you have to stop this investigation, because I will kill you if you keep this up."

"Nikki, the first domino has tipped already, there are too many big wigs involved in it now."

"I don't like talking in circles, I don't care who has to die. If this investigation keeps going on a lot of people are going to die, Captain. I don't want any problems, but trust me, I'm not the one people want problems with." Nikki picked up her cigar and relit it.

"You do know that your apes killed my dog?"

"Captain, they could have killed you as you stepped on the boat. It's time to walk on the deck, Captain," Captain Fuller got up and walked onto the deck, he felt the cool breeze as the air ghosted over his flesh. He looked at the Black Sea, the water was dark as night.

"So is this where you throw me overboard with brick tied to my ankles?" Nikki laughed.

"Captain, you have been watching too many mafia movies... just listen, you don't hear no cars or gunshots, the only noise you hear is the sound of the sea and it's so peaceful... come on our food is waiting for us." Captain Fuller sat at the table and talked with Nikki and shared a meal as Drama recorded everything from the laughing, to them smoking a cigar together. They stayed on the boat for about 2 hours before they dropped Captain Fuller off at his house, but he never knew that he was being recorded.

Chapter 10

Drama walked up to Mayhem and dapped him up as he smoked his blunt in the back of the auto parts shop.

"Yo, this nigga Cordell ain't living right... he's moving foul, word to my mother, son."

"Mayhem what the fuck you mean living foul you know how Nikki feel about that nigga." Mayhem pulled his blunt before talking

'I followed that nigga the other night down to the warehouse on the backside of Brooklyn." Drama looked at Mayhem not saying a word.

"That fool pulled up on Kareem and Jasmine, I don't know what they were talking about in the warehouse, but I do know what he went to meet up with them for."

"Why the fuck would he do that? That will be crossing Nikki out and gambling with his life."

"Because he believed that Nikki had something to do with Malachi getting bodied."

"Hell no, I can't go for that one baby boy. Why the fuck would he think that?"

"I don't know what the fuck was on that nigga's mind or why would he think that, but I could prove it."

"How is that?"Mayhem pulled his phone out and showed Drama the video of Cordell talking to Kareem over the phone.

"Fuck, this nigga just bodied himself."

THE BLACK DIAMOND CARTEL 3 | SAYNOMORE

"I already know shit is about to go 0 to 100 real fast." Drama shook his head and licked his lips.

"Come on, we need to show Nikki before she thinks we are part of this bullshit. I ain't trying to be strapped down to no fucking table or eaten by no fucking dogs alive."

"Yo, copy that. Let's pull up on her because I ain't trying to be butt ass naked with no pool stick up my ass, real talk. You know her mind is sick as hell."

***

It was raining outside as the car pulled up to the warehouse there were four guys standing outside the garage doors. The cars pulled inside the warehouse and Kareem stepped outside smoking a cigar as he walked up to the table where they were cutting up kilos of cocaine. On the table to the right of him they was counting stacks of money, 4 Tray walked up to him.

"Boss, you know we are ready to ride on Nikki and her apes."

"Yeah I know already, but we have one shot and we don't want to miss it."

"Alright, so where do we go from here?"

"It's a waiting game, we wait, we strike, we kill, we have somebody working on that now for us."

"So we going to play nice in the sandbox for now?"

"Yeah, just for now?"

***

Nikki was feeding both her dogs when Drama and Mayhem knocked at her office door she looked at both of her pit bulls before getting up to open the door.

"Stay, don't move."she walked to the door and opened it and looked at and in Mayhem.

"Come in, I just got done feeding my pups."Drama looked at Nicki and laughed.

"No disrespect Nikki, I done seen both of them killers eat motherfuckers alive, they ain't no damn puppies at all."

"Drama, no matter how old a boy gets to his mother he will always be her baby boy... just like a daughter will always be her father's little princess. So no matter how many people they kill they are always my puppies, okay?"

"Whatever you say Nikki."

"So tell me what's on your mind, what made you come to the office?" Drama took a deep breath before talking.

"Mayhem, let her know the business." Nicki looked at Mayhem.

"Yeah Mayhem, let me know the business."

"Real talk, I was smoking a blunt the other night... matter of fact it was the day y'all paid Captain Fuller a visit. I was on the side of the auto parts shop in the cut when Cordell pulled up back there talking on the phone, he couldn't see me... but long story short, he had a meeting with Kareem." Nikki cut him off.

"How do you know he had a meeting with Kareem?"

"Before you paid Captain Fuller a visit I followed him to the warehouse on the backside of Brooklyn, I saw Kareem talking with Jasmine and they were talking about Malachi's murder, they were saying you did it."

"Mayhem, I look at you as a son and I never question my apes, but how do I know the story you are telling me is true... how can you prove it?" Mayhem showed Nikki both videos on his phone. Nikki bit down on her bottom lip with the look of death in her eyes as she tapped her fingernails on her desk.

"Do you want us to roll him Nikki?"

"No that nigga is going to die my way, but first I'm going to use a pawn to kill a king. Mayhem, I want you with him everywhere he goes, and if has to take a piss I don't care if you have to hold his dick... be in there with him."

"Say less, I'm on it."

47

"Good, now both of you go, I have something to do," Drama and Mayhem walked out the office and both of her dogs came and laid their head on her lap as she patted them on their heads as she thought to herself.

Chapter 11

"Benny, are you ready to go see Nikki?" Benny stood up and put both of his hands in the air as he got out from the bar as he looked at Chin.

"Yeah let's go see her, I heard good things about her, that's the only reason I agreed to the meeting with her. If a nigga could take over Harlem like this with the right people behind him imagine how far she could go. We were running New York, Florida, the East Coast for years now, let's go see what this murdering nigga bitch had to offer us."

"Sure thing boss, after you."

***

"Yo Kidd, Drama is pulling up on the block." Kidd looked and saw the black on black Benz pulling up.

"Alright, let me go see what Drama has going on, post up I'll be right back." Drama stepped out the car and walked up to Kidd and dapped him up.

"What's the word Drama?"

"Same shit new day, making money and dropping bodies...usual shit we do. But I'm over here because Nikki sent me."

"And what is Ms. Gunz talking about... besides having a nigga killed?"

"You know that's her everyday language, but she needs you to play for the other team for a minute. You know how that shit goes, get close to the motherfuckers until its time to pop the bottle on them, you get me?"

"And who the fuck am I'm trying to get close to?"

"Kareem and Jasmine, two of Malachi's top killers. They have a crew in Brooklyn that has got shit on lock."

"So why doesn't Nikki just do what she do and have these niggas roll? Why the fuck do I got to get close to them?"

"Nigga all that had been worked out, now let me put it to you this way… stop fucking asking questions and do what the fuck I told you needs to be done. You are a pawn on this chess board and Nikki just moved you." Drama looked at at Kidd with hate in his eyes.

"Sayless, I'll be in touch man."

"Good, cuz she want to see what you see and hear what you hear, so keep your eyes open and ear to the ground."

"Already on it."

Drama turned around and walked back to his car as Kidd walked back to Sid.

"Yo, what that nigga talking about?"

"Just some work I have to put in. Come on, let's get back to the block and do what the fuck we were doing."

Chapter 12

"Nikki, they're here. There's three cars, eight of them all together." Nikki walked over to the window and looked at Benny and his men as they walked into her auto parts shop.

"Come Drams, let's go meet our guys… where are Shady and Mayhem at?"

"In the back of the auto part shop with Cordell, everybody is in place."

"Good," Benny walked into the auto parts shop right up to Nikki. He didn't care for Nikki, she was black and he didn't trust her any farther than he could throw her, he just knew she had a grip on New York and he needed her. Not only that, but he respected her reputation. Nikki walked up and out of respect kissed Benny on the cheek.

"Benny, thank you for coming to see me." Benny didn't say a word he took her hand and kissed it, showing her the same respect she just showed him.

"No Nikki, thank you for allowing me to come see you."

"Come, should we go talk in private?"

"That sounds like a good idea, after you."

***

Kareem picked up the phone and called Jasmine, after a few rings she picked up.

"Jasmine, Cordell was right he was telling the truth, they are here and she's having the meeting now."

"How many guys you have with you?"

"Just me, 4 Tray, and Youngin… why what you have in mind?"

"I'm thinking a drive-by when they come out, make it look like she set everything up, that would be a win-win for us."

"She has the block locked down, she's got guys posted up all over the block and so do the Italians. Four men out front holding impressive machinery, we won't make it off the block." Jasmine sat down in her chair and crossed her legs ass she took a sip of wine.

"Kareem, at this point in time how is Nikki moving? I don't have time for excuses, figure it out and get it done." Jasmine hung up the phone after saying that, she took another sip of her wine then place the glass down on the end table and went into a deep thought.

***

"Nikki, it has come to my attention that Mrs. Blanka is no longer sitting at the table with you and that you had Hardbody killed, and that you are at war with Malachi's old crew?"

"Benny Garcia, Mrs. Blanka did walk away from me after she gave me a untenable choice. I stand on loyalty to my apes, I know what I bring to the table so trust me I'm not afraid to eat alone. Dead or alive I'm loyal to mine, so when my driver Cali took his last breath, Hardbodywas already a deadman. Mrs. Blanka wanted to talk about the situation, but I wasn't with the chit chat so if I had to lose her support in order to kill Hardbody who sent his shooters at me, so be it. I stand on loyalty over mine, facts." Benny nodded his head out of respect.

"And what about the problem with Malachi's old crew?"

"Let me put it to you this way, I'm not the type who wants problems, but I'm not the one you want problems with. I have

52

a group of apes who will swing from a tree, beat on their chest and bring me back someone's head for proof of kill, Benny."

"Nikki, I like your energy. I'm going to open the pipelines for you for 30% of your profit every month from each state you move your product in and that my guys have to sign off, do you agree with my terms?" Nikki really wanted to test the waters and tell Benny 15% but she knew her place and who she was dealing with.

"Benny, thank you and I agree to your terms for 30%."

"That's good to hear," Benny got up as well as Nikki did and shook hands.

"Nikki, I'll be in touch." Nikki kissed Benny's cheek before he walked away with his men.

***

Kareem pulled his gun out and cocked it as he looked at 4 Tray and Youngin.

"Jasmine wants you to pop now, she ain't trying to hear nothing else."

"Kareem, don't you make the calls? She's sending niggas on a death trip, you got these crackers out here holding shit like World War III is about to pop off and Nikki's Gorillaz, as she calls her apes are deep as fuck out here on the block." Youngin' looked at 4 Tray and cocked his gun back as he was talking.

"Kareem, no disrespect... but you're talking too much. Jasmine want these crackers popped on, I'm about to eat on them now. Y'all better lace up, cuz I'm about to shoot."

"Youngin, chill. This cracker is coming out now, he's moving like he's the untouchable Don." 4 Tray said.

"Good, because it's time to go grocery shopping. Let's eat." Youngin put his hoodie on and opened up the SUV's doors and jumped out, gun in his hand yelling, "Bang, bang, motherfucker." Benny looked at Youngin as he pointed his gun at them and started firing at him. Benny's bodyguard jumped in front of him blocking the bullets from striking Benny, Men started firing back at Youngin', he ran behind the SUV as Kareem opened up the door shooting back at them. Drama looked at Nikki from the inside of the auto parts shop.

"You heard that?" Nikki pulled her gun out, "Come on, they are after Benny." Bullets were flying from everywhere, it was an all-out shootout. Roulette pulled her gun out and looked at 4 Tray shooting from the side of his SUV. Kareem looked at 4 Tray he went to yell but it was too late, he was dead in Roulette's eyes. He yelled "4 Tray!"

4 Tray turned around and looked at Roulette as the bullets were coming out of her gun and ripping his chest open. Nikki came out of the auto parts shop shooting at the SUV, alongside of Drama. Benny looked up at Nikki and Drama as he was getting up and going back into the auto parts shop Shady came outside shooting a M16. Roulette ducked for cover running a few cars down, Youngin ran up to 4 Tray and scooped him up and put him in the SUV. Kareem was shooting at everyone he seen as he jumped in the SUV and pulled off. The SUV was getting shot up as all the windows were shot out and holes peppered the doors. 4 Tray was taking deep breaths as Youngin and was putting pressure on his gunshot wound.

***

Nikki lowered her gun and walked into the auto parts shop, she looked at Benny and his dead guy on the floor. Benny walked up to Nikki and looked into her eyes.

"My man is dead, I was almost killed, and your city is tumultuous. Everything stops now until I see a body count on the news, and we find the one who sent the shooters... I want them fucking dead."

"Benny, I'm going to take care of it personally."

"Better sooner than later." Benny walked off with his man back to his car. Nicki looked at Cordell and Shady and Mayhem.

"Shady, you and Mayhem in my office now. Cordell, you and Drama clean this shit the fuck up before the police show up and start their bullshit."

Chapter 12

Jasmine watched as the black SUV pulled up with the broken windows, she watched as Youngin was helping 4 Tray out the SUV when Kareem walked over to her.

"Shit was real fucked up out there today, 4 Tray got clapped but Benny and Nikki got the message."

"Do they know it was us that sent the message?" Kareem looked at Jasmine but she thought before speaking,

"Passion played out, I know they know it was us, we didn't have a murder one mask over our face. I know Shady saw my face, this is what the fuck you wanted… guns up, it's crunch time should have got shot."

"I know it's crunch time, just make sure you ain't the one getting shot at Kareem."

***

"Shady, because I respect you I'm going to show you this video. Things could have went all wrong, only three people knew about this meeting today: me, you, and Cordell. Shady, Cordell is a fucking rat… he's a traitor and one of Benny's men was killed today. The pipeline is closed because of him."

"Wait Nikki, how do you know it was him? That nigga doesn't even move like that, I can't even picture him doing no crazy shit like that towards our apes, that's on my diamonds."

"Nikki, here is the phone?" Mayhem passed Nikki his phone, Shady looked at her then Mayhem.

"Sorry, sometimes the people you think you know only wore a mask. Cordell's mask came off and the man we thought we knew showed us a different face." Shady looked at the whole video and then back at Nikki and Mayhem he went to walk away when Nikki stopped them.

"The truth hurts but sometimes you got to learn the truth in order to move on from the past." Shady shook his head.

"Shady, there's more… come here." Shady turned around and looked at the video in the warehouse of Cordell talking to Kareem and Jasmine. Shady just dropped his head.

"Shady, I know how you feel about Cordell but you don't need to be there for this, there's only one way to make this right."

"Nikki, let me kill him… let me do it."Nicki looked at Mayhem when Shady said that, Mayhem shook his head saying no.

"Shady, you're not going to be there. I want you to go to the block and check on Roulette and Remy, make sure everything is smooth out there. I don't want you to see this, it's not going to be a quick death." Shady wiped his hand over his face and shook his head as he walked out the office. "Mayhem, follow him and if shit don't look right body his ass. I don't have the time for disloyal ass niggas in my circle."

"Okay, what about Cordell?" Nikki smiled as she lit her cigar.

"I already told Drama to make sure he doesn't move and to make the move on him. He should already be tied down or chained up to the ceiling in the back of the auto parts shop. Now go follow Shady as I take care of Cordell traitorous ass."

"Copy that," Mayhem said as he walked off.

***

Nikki walked into the back of the auto parts shop where she had 12 of her apes standing around looking at Cordell with his hands tied to chains hanging from the ceiling with just his boxers on. It was easy to tell he had been beat up very badly. Nikki walked past all her apes right up to Cordell and looked him in his eyes. She then turned around and looked at all of her apes, "This motherfucker right here is a disloyal son of a bitch. I welcomed him into my house, I gave him a home, I fed him, I made him into a made nigga and how the fuck does he repay me? By going to the ops and telling them about this meeting I had today. See I knew some funny shit was going on, so I only told two people about this meeting. Shady and this fucking traitor, Cordell, I told Shady the meeting was at 1:00 pm, next week and I told this pussy ass nigga Cordell the meeting was today at 4:00 pm and look what the fuck happened. Shit popped off today, niggas took shots at us today and almost fucked up what we have going on. So I'm going to show this traitor today before he takes his last breath what real pain feels like. Drama, go get that plastic and place it underneath him… it's going to get very bloody. One thing I did learn from Malachi is that loyalty comes with a price, and Cordell… your loyalty that comes with the price today that will be paid in all blood." Cordell looked at Nikki with the blood coming from his mouth.

"Fuck you Nikki, I know you killed Malachi… he was fucking loyal to you, you monkey bitch." he then spit the blood on the floor next to her feet, Nikki smiled.

"You disrespectful motherfucker, you must love pain but don't worry because what I'm going to do to you is going to get my pussy wet, that I promise you." Nikki walked up to the table and took her jacket off and placed it on the chair before she walked up to Cordell and grabbed his face by the chain. She took a straight razor she had from her pocket and cut his tongue out. Cordell was shaking and screaming as she cut his tongue out of his mouth, she had blood all over her hands and running down her arms. She turned around and looked at all of her apes as she held his tongue in her hand, she dropped it on the floor. Cordell was screaming out of pain.

"You bring me that baseball bat, it's time to have fun. Now Cordell, this is really going to hurt, I promise you that you fucking rat."

***

"Shady, hold up my nigga... let me get in your ear for a minute." Shady stopped and look at Drama.

"What's up?"

"Shady, I know how you feel right now, dead ass I do."

"Do you my nigga? Cordell showed me this game, put my first gun in my hand, my first pack to sell on the block. I caught my first body with Cordell and we took over New Jersey together, so don't tell me you know how the fuck I feel, because you don't. Let me show you something Drama," Drama looked at Shady as he pulled up his sleeve to his shirt and showed Drama the brand that consisted of three letters that said BDC. "Me and Cordell's relationship is deeper than what you think, Drama."

"So Shady, no disrespect... you know the rules in the streets better than anybody else. The rules of the cartel is that nobody is bigger than the cartel, and you know how Nikki is... how she runs the Blood Diamond Cartel." Shady shook his head.

"Look Drama, I just need some time to myself, I'm going to clap your line later."

"Yeah, do that bro. Love is love kid."

"Yeah, love is love." Drama just watching Shady walk on, shaking his head knowing they just asked that man to walk away while they killed someone who was more than just a friend, rather it was like Shady's brother.

Chapter 13

"Kareem, Nikki is a cold-hearted bitch, I want everything around her dead."

Jasmine looked at Cordell's dead body that had been beaten and chopped up in the brown casket that Nikki had delivered to them. The casket was full of rats, eating Cordell's body along with a note that had the date and time of the meeting she had with Benny.

"How are we going to do that Jasmine? Nikki is always two steps ahead of us, let's face the facts, now that she has the Louisiana Sicilian Mafia behind her you know what that means? More guns on top of more guns."

"Kareem, I have more guns too. Nikki isn't the only one who has friends. I have to go see someone, I'll be back in a few days." Jasmine looked at Cordell's body one more time before walking off.

"Jasmine, we are in the middle of a war that just started and you're telling me you'll be back in a few days?"

"Yeah, I'm going to get more guns like I said. Nikki isn't the only one with friends." Kareem looked inside the casket one more time at Cordell's dead body before walking off.

***

Private Investigator Oldham walked to his car with two bags in his hand as he was leaving the store. As he was opening his trunk he was smacked in the back of the head with the billy club knocking them out cold. He dropped his car keys on the ground as he was pushed in the trunk of the car, Mayhem picked the keys up and looked around before getting into the car and driving off. Drama looked at Nikki in the back seat of the Escalade as she watched everything as she smoked on her cigar.

"Drama take me to the docks, it's time that Mr. Oldham knows who the fuck he's dealing with."

"Yes ma'am," Nikki didn't say another word as Drama pulled off, headed to the docks.

***

Kareem walked up to Kidd as he stood next to his car, he had 4 Tray and Youngin with him.

"Is this the man I need to see right here? Is this the shot caller, the boss of bosses?" Kidd said as he was smiling and rubbing his hands together. "Yeah that's me, but see the problem is I don't know you. I don't know shit about you, so won't you tell me who the fuck you are and what I could do for you?"

"No disrespect, I was just trying to get some money with the winning team and how y'all living up here I could fit right in and stack my cash."

"Yo, Youngin, you know about this nigga?" Kareem looked over at Youngin.

"I don't know shit about this nigga, matter of fact this is the first time I seen this goofy ass nigga." Kareem looked at 4 Tray.

"What about you, 4 Trey?"

"Yeah I know this nigga, I seen him around the block making plays." Kareem nodded.

"So you put your stamp on this nigga?" 4 Tray looked at Kidd.

"Yeah, I stamped this nigga."

"Good, start him off with a couple of runs, and 4 Tray if he fucks up you are going to wish those bullets that went into your chest took your life." Kareem didn't say another word as he turned around and walked off with Youngin behind him. 4 Tray walked up to Kidd and looked him in the eyes.

"Yo, I gave you my stamp... don't fuck up and spill my blood nigga."

"Yo, you know I got you nigga, my word is my bond."

"Fuck your word, just prove it to me." Kidd nodded as 4 Tray walked off behind Youngin and Kareem

***

Investigator Oldham opened his eyes, everything was a blur to him. He had a pounding headache, he quickly took stock of his current predicament —his hands were tied down with chains attached to bricks, as well as his feet. He looked at Nicki smoking a cigar leaning against the edge of the boat.

"Mr Oldham, I hate to meet up like this under these circumstances but hey, shit happens. I would introduce myself but from the pictures and videos we got from your house you already know who I am, so let's talk shall we?"

"Am I going to die?"

"That's all up to you, Mr Oldham." and in the back of his mind he knew he was going to die.

"Why am I chained down if I'm not going to die?"

"I never said you weren't going to die... I said it's all up to you."

"Let's cut to the chase, what do you want from me?"

"Why have you been following me and who are you working for?"

"I'm not working for anybody," Nikki looked at Mayhem and nodded her head at him, Oldham looked at Mayhem pouring a bucket of blood over the edge of the boat Nikki looked at Drama,

"You're not going to talk for me, Drama… throw his ass overboard." Drama walked over to Oldham with Mayhem and picked up the chair Oldham was tied down to.

"Wait, wait I swear. I'm not working for anyone, I swear to fucking God I'm not."

Nikki held her hand in the air to stop them from throwing him overboard.

"Why shouldn't I kill you? What good are you to me?" "I can work for you, I'm fucking good at what I do. Look at everything I had on you that you didn't know about."

"Oldham, I'm going to let you live. Under these circumstances you will get your job back at the police station, you will let me know everything that's going on in there, do you understand me?" Nikki looked him in his eyes, they looked anxiously from right to left. Nikki knew that Oldham was a gamble that she could win or lose, the question became did she want to take that risk? This collaboration would be like playing with a double edged sword.

"I don't trust him, Drama toss his ass overboard." "No, no, no… wait, wait please, not like this, don't drown me I swear I won't cross you."

"I know you won't, because you only will have the fish to talk to." Nikki nodded at Mayhem and Drama and watched as they threw him overboard. All you heard was a splash of the water and Oldham hitting the water.

"Mayhem, when we get back to the docks I want you to go burn down Oldham's house, pour gas in every room of the house, just in case he has something in there that we haven't found."

"Okay, I'll do that as soon as I get back Nikki." "Good, Drama I need updates on Kidd, I need to know about his progress." Drama nodded.

"I'll get on that as soon as I get back."

"Good, I'll pull up on him as soon as we get back." Nikki walked to the table on the deck and sat down in a chair and lit her cigar. Things were certainly coming together.

Chapter 14

Jasmine's limo pulled up to the white fence at Garcia mansion. Mrs Blanka had guards everywhere holding M16 and AR-15s. When the guards opened the gate, the limo pulled up to the house. Mrs. Blanka walked up to the limo as Jasmine was getting out, she smiled and kissed her on the cheek.

"Jasmine, it is so good to see you again my child. Come have lunch with me, I have something prepared in the garden for us as we talk. Please, we have much to talk about."

"Yes we do, Mrs. Blanka." Mrs. Blanka walked Jasmine to the garden where there was a table set for them.

"So, tell me Jasmine, why did you come all the way down here to see me?"

Mrs. Blanka poured her a glass of green tea before Jasmine could say anything.

"Thank you for the tea, Mrs. Blanka."

"You're welcome, now tell me Jasmine. what is on your mind?"

"I need your help, Mrs. Blanka. You once said you owe me your life, now I'm asking you to help save mine." Mrs. Blanka nodded her head. "Nikki… you are asking me to kill her?"

"Yes, I am. She's becoming too powerful and I know she had Malachi killed on your orders."

"Jasmine, I owe you my life and I owe Nikki a debt as well. The debt I owe her your debt overrules, but yes, I did have Malachi killed for his disloyalty."

"But why? You never told me Mrs. Blanka that you had Malachi killed over his disloyalty."

"Because somethings are best left quiet. Jasmine, become my blood sister and pledge your loyalty and honor to me, and I will take care of Nikki. But only if you pledge your loyalty to me is the only way this is going to work."

"I pledge my loyalty to you, Mrs. Blanka." Mrs. Blanka looked at her waiter and waved him over, when he reached the table he placed the plate with a cover over it down on the table and pulled the lid off and there was a straight razor on the plate. Mrs. Blanka picked the razor up and cut her right hand, she didn't place the razor down and looked at Jasmine. Jasmine picked the razor up and and did the same thing, and she took her hand and place it in Mrs. Blanka's outstretched hand and looked in her eyes.

"Flesh of my flesh, blood of my blood. It that blood that makes you related, loyalty makes you family. We are bonded by blood and forged by loyalty, you are my sister and blood. Come now, let's talk about the the assassination of Nikki Gunz and how this will play out."

***

"What do we got here, Captain Fuller?"

"Looks to be a four-hour house fire that left us with nothing but a fucking pile of ashes, Chief."

"Do you know whose house this is Captain?"

"Yeah I do, it's Oldham's house."

"If they did this to his house then we are just waiting for someone to find his body."

"Yeah, that's going to be like finding a needle in a haystack, Chief,"

"I guess you need to get your best guys out there looking for that needle then, because whoever had his house burned down there's something they don't want us to find. So we find him we find a secret they don't want out."

Chief Ward looked around one more time before walking off, leaving Captain Phillips looking at a pile of ashes.

Chapter 15

Kareem sat at the edge of the desk smoking a cigar when his phone went off. He looked and seen it was Jasmine calling and he got off his desk and walked to the window and looked outside as he answered the phone.

"Jasmine, what you have for me?"

"Mrs. Blanka is going to take care of Nikki, she will be sending someone up there to take care of the job, he's a professional and good at what he does." "

"And in return, what do we owe her?"

"I gave her our loyalty, a blood oath... the same oath that Malachi gave her."

"So we are protected by the cartel now?"

"Yeah we also have a major supply of power coming our way, enough to take over the East Coast."

"And when is the shipment?"

"2 weeks from today."

"Good, I'll start getting things together up here." "Okay, I'll see you as soon as I get back." Jasmine hung up the phone and stepped out of the limo as she got on the private jet. Kareem walked to his desk and pulled out a picture he had with Malachi and looked at it.

"Malachi, what am I missing? What am I not seeing here? You would have been putting two and two together by now." Kareem put the picture back knowing their itches were about to get scratched.

***

Benny sat at the table smoking a cigar and reading a newspaper when Chin walked up to him and sat at the table.

"So, what are we going to do about this nigga Nikki? It's been 2 weeks and I haven't heard nothing about nothing yet boss." Benny calmly folded the newspaper and laid it down on the table and looked at Chin as he pulled the cigar. He pulled three pictures out of his jacket pocket and passed them to Chin.

"She found the rat that told whoever about our meeting and she cut his ass up alive. Then she put his body in a casket and covered it with rats, that is a strong message not only to her cartel but to whoever try to kill us. She gave me her word and she is taking care of it personally."

"So she doesn't know who tried to kill us and put Bernie in a casket?"

"Chin, a partnership comes with trust... let's trust Nikki and see how she takes care of this particular problem. Look at what she has accomplished already Chin."

"Yeah, I guess you are right boss. I'll cut her some slack... let's see what she could do."

"That's all I'm asking you Chin, to give her a chance." Chin knocked twice on the table and stood up.

"I'm about to go, I have a junkyard to run and check on the operation down there."

"Sounds good, keep me posted."

"Will do," Chin walked off as Benny picked his newspaper back up and tucked the pictures back in his jacket pocket.

Chapter 16

Drama walked up to Nikki as she sat in the backyard of her mansion looking at her dogs running around playing with a rope.

"Nikki, you wanted to see me?" Nikki placed her hand on the bench next to her, giving a sign for Drama to sit down next to her.

"Drama, I haven't killed a lot of people in the worst way all because what Malachi did to me, but I also have a very good heart. I have helped so many people that couldn't help themselves or their families, so I step in and did what they couldn't and I made a lot of friends that way."

"Nikki, can I ask you something?"

"Go ahead."

"Did you do it?"

"Do what?"

"Kill Malachi."

"Drama, Malachi had me beat, raped, and branded. He had me killing innocent people, he had me selling drugs, he dogged me the fuck out and he broke me down to my lowest point of life. He threatened my family while he took my life from me. So I played under him and won his trust, he gave me his support to start my own family and when his guard was down, I killed him. I shot him dead in the face and then I stood over his body and shot him three more times, now you know why I killed Malachi."

"I understand, I would have killed him too after all of that."

"Drama… he put me in a position to help others and I did, I helped families come to America and because of that I made friends, and one of them reached out to me yesterday and told me that Jasmine went to see Mrs, Blanka and they took a blood oath with each other. The same one Malachi did, and Mrs. Blanka is sending someone up here to kill me, she told me."

"Do you believe her?"

"100% I do, and I need you to have everyone minding their p's and q's."

"You know I'm already going to do that, I'm going to take care of that now."

"I know, and that's why I put my trust in you, Drama."

"What about Kareem and the others? What are we going to do with them?"

"Let's just see what Kidd comes up with first before we strike."

"I'll keep you posted."

"Good." Nikki called her dogs over to her and started playing with them as Drama walked off.

Chapter 17

"Carlos, our friend Nikki needs to die. Jasmine will meet you in America so you can do what you do best for me."

"Mrs. Blanka, is there any type of way you want her to die?"

"Do whatever you need to do in order to get the job done." "Yes ma'am, I'll get on it right away."

"I know you will, your plane leaves tomorrow. "

"Yes ma'am." Mrs. Blanka walked up to Carlos and kissed his right cheek before walking off. Cynthia was planted in the garden and she heard everything that Mrs. Blanka said to Carlos before walking off, just like she had heard everything and saw everything when Jasmine was talking to Mrs. Blanka in the garden.

Chapter 18

Youngin was smoking a blunt and riding around with 4 Tray in the black on black BMW playing Jay-Z's *Rock Boys* when suddenly Youngin saw Roulette talking to Remy on 127th and Park.

"Yo, 4 Tray... ain't that that bitch that tried to flatline you over there in the pink and white?"

"Yo bro, I'm about to pop the bottle on that hoe right now." 4 Tray put his gun out and cocked it back as he watched Roulette and Remy walk towards the light.

"Remy, Drama just texted and said there's an emergency meeting right now." Remy looked at her phone as well.

"I just got that same text Roulette, something big must be going down. Come on, let's get to the auto parts shop now." Roulette stopped walking when she saw the black on black BMW doors open and 4 Tray jumped out holding a black 9 mm pointed at her. "What's up now bitch?" Before Roulette could pull her gun out 4 Tray was already letting bullets rip through her chest. Remy pulled her gun out and started shooting at the black BMW as 4 Tray jumped back in the car as Youngin pulled off. Remy ran up to Roulette and was holding her hand as she laid in a pool of blood, looking up at her sightlessly.

"Roulette, hold on, fight this... don't die on me, fight this baby you got this." Roulette tried to say something as blood bubbles were coming out of her mouth, then her eyes just stared into space at that point. Remy knew she was dead. She picked Roulette's gun up and took off running, everyone watched Roulette laying in a pool of her own blood because she was caught off guard and there was nothing she could do to fight fate.

***

"Yo, y'all listen up… we've been holding Harlem down for 5 years now, going toe to toe against every fucking body. Nikki calls us her apes and our language in the streets is a fucking body count. We don't do the chit chat, Hardbody sent his shooters and he got fucking rolled. So we need new laws on the block pre Nikki, if they ain't one of us…then body them. Everyone will wear gray flags so we know who is who, don't have a gray flag, wear a gray shirt or fitted hat. I don't give a fuck just make sure you have gray on. I look around and see everybody but Remy and Roulette. Does anybody know where the fuck they are?" That was when Remy walked into the back doors, all eyes were on her she was covered with Roulette's blood. Shady walked up to her, "Remy, what the fuck happened?" Drama walked from the front of the room as well.

"Them niggas from the other day with the shoot out, pulled up on the block in a black BMW and rolled out. They bodied Roulette, I shot the car up but they killed her." Drama looked at Shady and Mayhem, "Get the apes together, find out where Kareem is and then body his ass. I need to call Nikki, Brooklyn is about to know what the fuck Harlem is talking about."

Chapter 19

"This is Barbara Wright with Channel 5 Action News, we are breaking in live with a breaking news report of a currently unfolding situation. There has been another mass shooting in Brooklyn, at a nightclub where we were told three are dead and four others are wounded. Last week there was another fatal shootout, it appears both are related to a ongoing turf war. If you remember we reported on a shootout in Harlem that happened two days ago. Two officers arrived on the scene and entered the ongoing shootout, one officer was shot with non life threatening injuries, no one was arrested. This is becoming the worst summer in New York history. NYPD Chief Ward is offering a $50,000 reward for any information leading to an arrest, you can call the Crime Stoppers hotline, all phone calls are kept confidential. Stay tuned for further updates, this is Barbara Wright with Channel 5 Action News, we now return you to your regularly scheduled programming."

***

Nikki cut the TV off and looked at Captain Fuller as she lit her cigar.

"What are you going to do about this Captain, or do I have to take care of her myself? She can go on a boat ride, you know I don't mind."

"Nikki, she is just a news reporter… she is doing her job, what do you want me to do?"

"Captain Fuller, I don't give a fuck what you say to her… just make sure that bitch keeps her mouth closed. No doubt I will put her ass on the front page of the newspaper asking "Have you seen me?" Test my gangster and she will be missing by tonight."

" Nikki, I'm here to ask you one question."

"And what's that Captain?"

"It's about Detective Oldham, do you know or did you have your hands involved with his missing person case?" "Captain, let the case go cold… it's best for everyone or more bodies might drop." Nikki reached into her desk drawer and pulled out $10,000 in a white envelope and slid it to Captain Fuller.

"Nikki, I didn't come here for that."

"Captain Fuller, you are on my payroll… take the money and shut the bitch up. I don't like repeating myself." Captain Fuller got up and walked out leaving Nikki in her office. Nikki turned around and cut the news back on the TV to finish watching the update.

***

Jasmine looked out the window as Carlos' car pulled up to the front of the building. She watched her guys open the door for him to step out the limo, she walked to the bar and got three glasses and a bottle of Ciroc and placed it on the table. Carlos walked in the office and Jasmine gave him a hug and a kiss on the cheek out of respect. "Carlos, thank you for coming."

"No problem, Jasmine. Mrs. Blanka told me about the former friend we must lay down."

"It's sad," Jasmine said as she walked to the table and picked up the bottle and poured everyone a shot of Ciroc, "It is sad, but these situations must be resolved, there's nothing you can do but put a mad dog to sleep."

"That is true, and so do you know where can I find this mad dog at?"

"Let's have a drink then we can go over the details later."

"And what are we drinking to Jasmine?"

"A dead bitch," Everyone smiled and tapped their glasses.

***

"Jasmine is making a move, Shady. I need to know that I could trust you, that if it came down to me and her then I could trust you would push the button on her to save my life."

"Nikki, I've been by your side from day one after Malachi's murder. I never went against you I just killed seven people in the last three weeks over you, I have killed more people that I could ever count over the last 6 years. Nikki, my breaking point was when I saw the way you took out Cordell. I'm not taking Jasmine's side over yours, I'm just asking for my walking papers. I want to be free of the Blood Diamond Cartel. I want to make my own amends with God. I'm done, Nikki." Nikki look at Shady as he took his gun off his hip and set it on the table. "Shady, you say you want to make your own amends with God... do you pray, Shady? To God I mean?"

Shady took a deep breath.

"Over the last few weeks I have been praying day and night, fighting my demons." Nikki closed her eyes and then cut them at Drama. Nikki licked her lips and nodded her head, she walked up to Shady and kissed him on the cheek and then his forehead.

"Shady, I don't fight my demons anymore, I make friends with them. But if you want to leave, go make your amends with God and find your peace." Shady knew in his heart he was going to die, but if that was how he was going to find his peace let that be the reason. He took his last breath as he turned around to walk away. Nikki pulled her gun and pointed at the back of his head. Drama turned his head and closed his eyes as the sound of the gunshot reverberated through the office, dropping Shady to the ground. Nikki walked over to Shady's dead body and looked down at him.

"Now you can make your amends with God face to face, and you're free now from the Blood Diamond Cartel. Drama, make sure you bury him next to Malachi and get someone to clean his body up."

"I got you, Nikki." Drama looked at Shady one more time, knowing his little man was ready to die by telling Nikki he was done with the Blood Diamond Cartel, she made it very clear that there was only one way out and she stood on it period.

***

Captain Fuller walked in Chief Ward's office and sat down in front of his desk, he looked at him and then placed the pen he had in his hand down on the desk before he leaned back in his seat.

"Talk to me Captain, what's on your mind?"

"For us to get Nikki we need the media to be quiet, they'll give her a heads up."

"Captain, that's her job… now what progress do you have? Have we uncovered the whereabouts of former detective Oldham?"

"Chief, we both know he's dead, we are simply looking for a dead body at this point in time."

"I know you are right, I guess I have to face the fact. Who do you think is behind this?"

"Who else, Chief? Nikki Gunz is responsible."

"Here's the thing, there are no leads to find his body. But if we can pin anything regarding his murder on Nikki and everything else that will be a big ass win for us."

"How are you going to do that? She is very protective, we don't know who she has in her back pocket... who's working for her... these are the questions we need answers to, Chief."

"Yeah I know, I'll make some calls and I'll reach out to you in a little while."

"Okay, I'll be waiting to hear from you." Captain Fuller glanced at Chief Ward as he picked up the phone and made a call before leaving his office.

Chapter 20

Carlos sat three buildings down from Nikki's auto parts shop with an assault rifle laid across his lap. He's been there for the last 2 hours waiting for Nikki to come out, Youngin and 4 Tray were with him just in case anything went wrong. There were people on the streets smoking blunts, playing music, drinking, rolling dice... but none of that distracted Carlos, he never took his eyes off of the entrance of Nikki's shop. That's when he saw the doors open, in a deep Hispanic accent he said.

"I think this is her coming out, get ready because it's about to go down... one mad dog is about to be killed."

"Carlos, remember what Jasmine said... shoot her in the chest because she wants to go to the funeral and look down at Nikki's face in the casket just like she did Malachi and tell her how much she fucking hates her."

"I know already, 4 Tray." Carlos looked at Nikki as she walked out of the auto parts shop with Drama, "Nikki, I don't think we should be out here like this... it's too dangerous right now, we have too many enemies aiming at us and this ain't smart."

"Drama, whatever's going to happen is going to happen, I'm not running from no one.". Before Drama could say another word all they heard was the echo of the gun blast and then they saw Nikki's body being blown back from the impact of the bullet. Drama looked at Nikki's body laying on the ground. Mayhem ran out to Drama as they ran over to Nikki's body.

"Bro, she ain't breathing... help me get her up into the car. We got to get into the hospital, she can't die like this." Mayhem and Drama got her body in the car, Drama jumped in the driver seat and pulled off doing 80 miles an hour headed towards the hospital.

"Nikki, look at me... look at me." was all Mayhem kept saying as he was headed to the hospital.

***

Jasmine looked at Youngin then at 4 Tray as they walked into the club and up to where she and Kareem were sitting.

"So is she dead?"

"Judging from the way her body jerked from the impact of that bullet and the way it hit her that bitch is dead. There ain't no coming back from that one, ain't no way." Jasmine looked at Kareem with a smile on her face before walking away. Kareem walked up to Youngin and 4 Tray.

"Y'all drop Carlos at the airport?"

"Right at the private jet. I watched him board it myself."

"Good, Nikki's dead so it's time to start the takeover. Y'all get ready to eat." Kareem walked off as he pulled his phone out and made a call.

***

Drama looked at everyone with hate in his eyes and his gun in his hand.

"It's up, do y'all understand what the fuck I'm saying? I don't have any understanding for shit like this. I want blood in the streets now... Kareem done fucked up and Jasmine is a dead bitch. We don't back down from nobody, we are the Blood Diamond Cartel and everybody's is on the menu right now. I don't have any love for the streets and that's a cold fucking fact." Drama looked at Remy, walking over to him she had her gun pressed to the back of a nigga's head. walking right to Drama as she told him.

"Get on your fucking knees." Drama approached Remy asking, "Who the fuck is this nigga?"

"He's one of Kareem's boys. He said he had a message for you from Kareem." Drama smiled when she said that.

"Kareem sent you to die motherfucker, you ain't in Brooklyn no more... this is Harlem baby."

"Look Kareem wants to talk to you, I have him on the line right now, the phone is in my top pocket." Drama took his phone from his pocket and held it to his ear.

"You know you sent this nigga to die right?"

"Ain't nobody else got to die, that's the point of this conversation so we can get an understanding with each other."

"Nigga, fuck your understanding. I want blood." Mayhem walked over to Drama and said something to him in his ear. Drama looked at him and nodded.

"Okay, let's meet up tomorrow night... neutral territory."

"How does Manhattan sound to you, 9:00 pm?" "That'll work, I'll be there and what about my man?" "He's good, I'm going to send this nigga back to you now."

"I'll see you tomorrow night." Drama gave him back the phone.

"Get this nigga the fuck out of here now."

"Kareem is going to meet us tomorrow night at the park, we are going to lay the terms out. It's going to be a deal or no deal, if there's a deal they'll walk out alive. No deal, the motherfuckers are dead tomorrow night and they'll go to see Nikki."

"Good, I can't wait to get this shit over with and look down at that bitch's dead body." Jasmine said with a smile on her face.

Chapter 21

Carlos walked up to Mrs. Blanka he set his bags down on the ground as Mrs. Blanka took both hands and placed them on his face and kissed his cheeks.

"Tell me Carlos, how did it go?"

"As planned, the mad dog was put to sleep as you requested."

"Good, now come have a drink with me in the garden we have much to talk about for what happens next."

***

Captain Fuller walked up to Mac as he was in the locker room at the precinct. Captain Fuller closed and locked the locker room door. He walked up to Mac as he was getting his things out of the locker.

"Mac, I'mma cut right to the point... where is Nikki? She's been gone for the last few days." Mac closed his locker and looked at Captain Fuller. "Sir, all I know is the reporters are saying she was shot, no one has heard from her since."

"Mac, cut the bullshit with that okay? I know you work for her, see the thing you keeping on forgetting is that we've been on to you for years now, hoping that you would be the missing link to put that murdering bitch behind bars. We've known you've been tipping her off."

" Sir, with the most respect... I really don't know what you're talking about." Captain Fuller smiled and pointed at

Mac, he then reach in his top pocket and pulled out some photos and passed them to Mac, "Maybe these will refresh your memory." Mac looked down at the pictures then back at Captain Fuller.

"So where do we go from here?" Mac sat down on the bench as he handed Captain Fuller the pictures back. Captain Fuller sat down next to Mac, "Now we move forward as one, if she is still alive we bring her ass to justice because she's got me by the balls, just like everyone else squeezing my nuts harder. So what do you say we bring this bitch to justice and burn everything she has down to the fucking ground?"

"Yeah Captain, let's roast this bitch." Captain Fuller put his hand out for Mac to shake it Captain Fuller and Mac shook hands with a smile on their faces.

"Good, now we've got a lot to talk about on how to get this bitch in cuffs, so tell me everything you know about her."

***

"So what's the word Kidd? What the ops talking about?" Kidd pulled on his blunt as he stood behind the auto parts shop talking to Mayhem and Drama. "It's a setup, word is already out about Nikki getting bodied so they are going to come to you with the deal, and if you turn it down they're going to fire off on y'all right then and there. Real talk you are going to get down with them or you going to lay down right then and there." Drama looked at Mayhem.

"Don't worry, we are going to be there after Nikki's service and see what the fuck these washed up Don's have to say." Kidd passed the blunt to Drama.

"Yo, when is the service for Nikki, Drama?"

"Next week, but it's a private service… it's not open to the public. Family only, and when I mean family, I'm talking about the Blood Diamond Cartel."

" Niggas have to respect that, so how much longer do I have to play undercover?"

" Just a little while longer, then you can come back home to the family."

"Cool, let me go finish my runs. I have some more drop-offs to make." Kidd dapped Drama and Mayhem up before walking off.

"Drama, at least we know it's a setup now."

"Yeah, but the good part is that we know now... so we can have our shooters in place."

"Fucking right, Blood Diamond shit."

Chapter 22

"Benny, word is that Nikki Gunz is dead. Killed by one of them Blanka shooters as a favor to Jasmine and Kareem, after they exchanged a blood oath." Benny swung his golf club hitting the ball and watching as it landed a few feet away from the hole and then looked back at Chin.

"Chin, people fall down all the time. Nikki was like no other, I would say that it's sad she died, but Mrs. Blanka had her own son killed—she is a cold hearted female and when she pushed the button people die. Her money is powerful and she has a lot of friends in high places. Nikki had a chance if you ask me, but she didn't see it coming."

"So where do we go from here?"

"I'm going to continue playing my rounds of golf like I set out to do earlier today and like I always say people die all the time and Nikki is just another dead body that Mrs. Blanka can add to her graveyard and it's sad because I really liked Nikki. I saw a bright future doing business with her now, so if you will excuse me I have a round of golf to finish." Chin walked up leaving Benny playing golf with his associates.

***

Jasmine sipped on a glass of wine when Kareem walked in the door he walked up to her and picked up a bottle of

Ciroc and a glass. He poured himself a strong drink then walked over to Jasmine.

"I just got word that Nikki is having a private service, family only...and when they mean family they're talking about the Blood Diamond Cartel, no one from the general public whatsoever." Jasmine took another sip of her wine before talking.

"I might not get the pleasure of seeing that bitch dead in a fucking casket but at least I can get the pleasure of knowing she is fucking dead." Jasmine plunked her glass down on the table and walked over to Kareem and kissed his lips. It only took a moment before passion caught and she started kissing his neck.

Kareem looked down at Jasmine and placed her on the table and started kissing all over her body as he slid her pants off. Jasmine let out a light moan as Kareem's tongue slinked its way into Jasmine's wet, warm box as he sucked on her clit. She wrapped her legs around his head and her hands were on his head as she was rotating her hips around as his tongue was deep inside of her. Jasmine pulled Kareem up by his shirt and started kissing him with a deep passion as she unbuttoned his pants and grabbed his manhood and place it inside of her. She let out a loud moan as he pushed himself inside of her his tongue was wrapped around hers.

"Baby, your dick is breaking my walls... fuck daddy, you're deep inside of me."

"Whose pussy is this? Tell me baby, whose your Daddy?"

" This is your pussy, I'm cumming Daddy!" Kareem started fucking Jasmine harder as her nails were digging along of his back.

"Baby, I'm about to cum all over the thick dick of yours."

"Go ahead, come on Daddy's dick beautiful... cum for me, cum all over Daddy's dick."

Jasmine started shaking as she started cumming all over Kareem's dick. Kareem pulled his dick out and looked at Jasmine.

"You done got me weak in the knees baby, facts."

" I felt when you came inside of me, Daddy. You cum hard inside this pussy and you had a big load."

"You bring it out of me," Jasmine looked at Kareem and smiled as she looked at her phone when it was going off on her desk. She got up and walked over and picked it up to see that Mrs. Blanka was calling her.

"Hello, Mrs. Blanka."

"Good afternoon, my child. I'm calling to let you know that your shipment will be there tomorrow night at 8:00 pm, the same location we talked about."

"I'll be waiting, and I will call you as soon as I receive it."

"Good, I'll be waiting to hear from you Jasmine."

"I'll be in touch." Jasmine hung up the phone and looked at Kareem as he was finishing his drink.

"We have a large shipment coming in tomorrow night, 400 kilos." Kareem walked over to Jasmine and kissed her lips.

"Let the takeover start, baby. Let the takeover start."

Chapter 23

There were two pictures of Nikki in the front of the church, and a red and gold iron between them ...there was a crowd of 80 plus and all of them were her apes and friends of Harlem. Everyone had gray on, there were two baskets in the front full of red and white roses... the pastor was at the front of the church and everyone was quiet as he began to speak. That's when Captain Fuller and Chief ward walked into the church, the pastor noticed them and continue to talk:

"Nikki to some was a brutal murderer who they couldn't wait to see burn in Hell for all eternity. But she was an angel to some of us... you can't clean the streets up without getting your hands dirty. Let me say that again, you can't clean the streets up without getting your hands dirty. They say, and I said they say she was a killer, she was a murderer. But what I didn't hear them say is how she paid for the kids and residents of Harlem to go to college, and how many jobs she provided the community... how she cleaned the streets up in Harlem. But they didn't say all of that, you have kids riding their bikes up and down the streets... now parents aren't worried about them getting shot no more. When was the last time police were around here harassing black people?" Drama got up and placed another basket down in front of the pastor as he was talking then he went back and took his seat.

"The basket here is to show Nikki the same love she showed our young brothers and sisters. Whether it folds or jingle, it will be appreciated." one by one people got up and made their way to the big basket and placed money into it. The pastor looked up above the balcony of the church and spotted someone up there, dressed all in black looking down. He couldn't tell who it was, he took his eyes off them for a second and when he looked back up they were gone.

"As I was saying, Nikki was a breath of fresh air to Harlem. She cleaned the streets up and did what the NYPD couldn't do. Whether it was by force or not she did it, she cleaned these streets up and she will be missed... she was a blessing and she was an angel to us. She will be missed she was loved." The service was 2 hours long. Drama was leaving Captain Fuller and Chief Ward stopped him.

"Drama, you have our deepest condolences about Nikki, she was like no other."

"No, she wasn't... she was the real one and she could never be replaced Captain."

"So I'm guessing you're the new head nigga in charge?" Drama laughed it off with a smile.

"Chief Ward, Captain Fuller, y'all have a nice day. I have to get going, take care." Drama walked pased them as he headed out the door of the church. "Captain, keep your eye on him because he isn't as smart as Nikki and if we can't get her, we'll put that son of a bitch behind bars. I'll find the buy money and I'll make that shit stick."

***

Kareem walked up to Youngin as he was smoking his cigar. "Youngin, how that shit looking?" Youngin looked at the containment unit and the pilot full with cocaine then he smiled at Kareem.

"Like butter baby, this shit looks better than pussy."

"I know that's right," Kareem pulled out his phone and called Jasmine. After a few rings she picked up, "Everything is good down here on the docks, we are about to start loading the shipment up into the trucks, headed towards the warehouse soon and everything is smooth."

"Good, let me call Mrs. Blanka now."

"Okay, I'll keep you posted when we get to the warehouse."

" I'm calling her now, I'll talk to you then." as he hung up the phone with Kareem she called Mrs. Blanka after a few minutes she picked up the phone.

"Hello Jasmine, I'm taking it everything is good?" "Yes, Mrs. Blanka, I'm calling to let you know everything is good on my end."

"Good, I'll be in touch." Mrs. Blanka hung up the phone and went to go pray to Santa Maria for watching over her and all her associates.

Chapter 24

"Guys are getting ready for tomorrow night, it's going down big... either these motherfuckers are going to get down or they going to lay down period." "Youngin, five niggas put them in Flatbush, 4 Tray you going to Brownsville everyone else stay close to where you been at we're going to do this like never before we are the Black Diamond Cartel. We are stamped from Malachi and blood and because of Jasmine now y'all motherfuckers are get ready to eat for real." 4 Tray walked up to Kareem after he finished talking."

"You might not care, but I thought I'd let you know I really didn't know how to tell you this but word just got back to me that your little homie, Shady... Nikki rolled him Kareem looked at 4 Tray and shook his head.

"Why he get rolled?"

"Word is, Nikki bodied him after she shared Cordell's he pulled up trying to balance she wasn't going for it she push that nigga shit back"

"Real talk, I appreciate you pulling up and letting me know about baby boy."

"Always fam." Kareem dapped 4 Tray up before walking off.

***

"Carlos, come walk with me to Santa Maria, it's time I go pray to her." Mrs. Blanka wrapped her arm around Carlos' arm as he walks her to the garden where she pray at he then looked at the night sky as Mrs.Blanka lit the candles around Santa Maria.

He looked at her one more time before walking off and leaving her to pray at the back of her mansion... he walked off far enough to give her respect as she prayed but close enough to watch her he was so focused on miss Blanko he didn't see the black figure coming up behind him dressed in all black they pulled the black nine millimeter out and pointed it at his head with the silencer on it. They'll pulled the trigger dropping him to the ground and then they stood over his body and pulled the trigger two more times. Making sure he was dead before they walked to the garden where Mrs. Blanka was at, as she was on her knees praying they looked at her quietly not saying a word as they pulled a knife out and popped it open before they walked behind Mrs. Blanka and grabbed her by the hand before they cut her throat from ear to ear then... they pushed her body down to the bottom of the statue. Mrs, Blanka had her hands on her throat coughing up blood she rolled over and looked at the person with the knife in their hand as blood was dripping off of it, they pulled their mask off so Mrs. Blanka could see their face before she took her last breath... the last face she saw looking down on her was Nikki holding a bloody knife in her hand. Nikki closed the knife and put the mask back on and walked out of the garden, leaving Mrs. Blanka laying a thick pool of blood laying under the statue of Santa Maria.

Chapter 25

Everyone was at the auto parts shop getting ready for the meeting in Manhattan when the back of the auto parts shop doors opened. Everyone looked lost as if they just seen a ghost as Nikki walked through the doors holding a double plated bulletproof vest in her hand. She walked up to Drama and gave him a kiss on the cheek, she did the same thing with Mayhem as she laid the bulletproof vest down on the table and looked at everyone.

4 Weeks Earlier: Before the Murder of Garcia Blanka
Nikki's black Range Rover pulled over on the back road in Brooklyn, Drama and Mayhem stepped out of the SUV with guns in their hand as Kidd walked over to them with a black hoodie on. He walked up the Drama and dapped him up as Mayhem opened the truck door for him to get inside. Nikki looked at him intently

"Kidd, tell me what you have to tell me and why I had to come into Brooklyn to meet with you face to face?"

"They just called a meeting for all of us…" Nikki held up a hand and cut him off.

"Who is they Kidd?"

"Kareem and Jasmine."

"Okay, continue… I'm listening."

"Mrs Blanka has a large shipment of cocaine coming within the next few weeks… over 400 kilos of cocaine. After they told us our parts we were all playing Jasmine dismissed all of us except for 4 Tray and Youngin. I walked around to the back of the room so I could hear what they was talking about, everyone was gone and I heard another voice with a heavy Spanish accent. Jasmine introduced him as Carlos." Nikki cut them off.

"You said Carlos?"

"Yes ma'am, I wanted to see how he looked so I cracked the door open a little more, he was tall and slim, dark brown." Nikki pulled her cigar before talking.

"I know who he is, Mrs. Blanka's assassin. If he's up here it's on Garcia Blanka's orders."

"Yeah, because he came up here to kill you for Jasmine as a personal favor for Mrs. Blanka to her."

"So when is this taking place? Did they say?"

"He told her it would be done in three days... however there's one thing that Jasmine told him."

"And what is that?"

"Do not shoot you in the face, she wants to look at your dead body in a casket as you did Malachi. He told her the gun he is using will rip your chest apart. Then she said something about a building across the street from the auto parts shop, then my phone started going off so I got out of there before I was seen."

"Thank you for this information Kidd, when this is over I will move you up in the ranks... just keep me posted on everything."

"Yes Nikki." Nikki gave Kidd her direct phone number before she tapped on the window for Drama to open the door for him to step out of the truck. Once he was out of the truck Mayhem and Drama got back in the truck Drama looked at Nikki.

"So do you believe his story?"

"Yes, I do. Genesis called me a few days ago and told me that Jasmine was down there and that she made a blood oath with Mrs. Blanka."

"Who is Genesis?"

"She was a female who I helped her family get up here from Mexico. She became a very close friend of mine. I just didn't want to believe what she said because I looked at Mrs. Blanka as a mentor, she showed me the ropes to be the apex predator that I am, now I have to kill her." Nikki didn't say anything else as she rode back to Harlem.

The Day Before the Shooting

"Nikki, Kidd was right, a Spanish man and two more dudes just went into the building. Mayhem just called me he's on his way back now."

"Good let's get this over with... help me put this bulletproof vest on."

"Nikki, this is crazy. I say let's just run up in there and kill them motherfuckers all at once."

"Drama, the cartel is involved now... they still are going to come at me. This is a blood oath, the only way they stop coming at me if they think I'm dead. So for me, to kill them they must think I'm dead." Mayhem walked in the doors as Drama was helping Nikki put on the bulletproof vest.

"Yo Nikki, you sure about this?" Mayhem asked her, "Mayhem, my plan is going to work... if this don't go right, Drama, you are the head, and Mayhem you are his number two. Now let's get this over with." Nikki gave Drama a hug and a kiss on the cheek. She did the same thing with Mayhem, she loved Mayhem... cuz she looked at him as if she was his mother, and he was her child he was young and hungry and she loved that about him.

"Now you have to remember everything I just told you to do, no shortcuts and do what I say and this is going to work."

The Night of Garcia Blanka's Murder

Genesis walked up to Nikki and gave her a hug, "Nikki, it is so good to see you again. I missed you so much."

"I miss you too, thank you for all your help."

"You helped my family... when everyone else looked down on us you saw us as humans and not dogs or slaves, my sister you will always be... now come on, I can sneak you in the back of the shed, nobody ever goes back there. Mrs. Blanka is out with Carlos and some of her guards are with her, so it's good to get you back there now."

"Let's go then." Genesis walked Nikki to the shed and closed the door once she was inside.

"Genesis, why is there so much dried up blood on the floor?"

"8 years ago, Malachi found out that Mrs. Blanka's son had his brother killed due to his actions, and killed his son that same day. Malachi found out the truth and had brought Manny back here. When Mrs. Blanka found out and she killed her son in that very spot, she had his wife take the kill shot. A few years passed and his wife couldn't take it no more and she came in here one rainy night and killed herself, since then nobody has came in here at all Nikki."

"So how is this going to work out tonight?"

"Nikki, every night at 8:00 pm Mrs. Blanka goes to the garden to pray with only Carlos as a personal security guard. He stands next to the oak tree every night, come look so you can see the path... you see the path?"

"Yeah I do."

"It's clean, there's no leaves or sticks, nothing to make noise when you walk, take it to the oak tree. Carlos won't see you coming, nor Mrs. Blanka. Then walk to the far part of the yard to go up that hill in a car, we'll be right there waiting for you."

"Thank you so much Genesis, this means so much to me."

"No, thank you... remember 8:00 pm, don't be late." Nikki kissed her one more time before she walked off, leaving Nikki in the shed. That night at 8:00 pm Nikki watched Carlos and Mrs. Blanka just like Genesis told her and everything was to the letter. After Nikki killed them she followed the path like Genesis told her and she was gone like she was never there. Leaving Garcia Blanka with her throat cut from ear to ear and Carlos with a bullet in the back of the head.

Present Day
"As I stand here, and looking at all of you I see a winning team who don't fold. When everyone thought I was dead I had to play the role, I did my job so we could win. I went to Mexico and killed Garcia Blanka myself. I cut her throat from ear to ear, when you fuck with us the only way out is death, period." At that point Drama turned the news on they were running the story of Mrs. Blanka's murder.

"Sorry to interrupt your regular scheduled programming, this is Barbara Wright with Channel 5 Action News we are bringing you a live update last night, notorious drug lord over the deadliest cartel in Mexico, Garcia Blanka was found dead with her throat cut from ear to ear as she was praying in her garden. Her body was discovered last night by her security team, for those of you who don't know who Garcia Blanka was she was the head of the dominant cartel in Mexico, her list of crimes include: she has ordered multiple assassinations and had tons of cocaine shipped all over the globe. Her cartel was responsible for extortion, murder, sex trafficking, and much more. At this point the police are not sure who is responsible for her murder. We will let you know more about Garcia Blanka's murder as it unfolds. This is Barbara Wright with Channel 5 Action News we now return you to your regularly scheduled programming."

***

Jasmine couldn't believe what she was hearing, the head of the deadliest cartel murdered at her own house with her throat cut from ear to ear. She looked at Kareem, she was lost for words. "Kareem, you have to be fucking kidding me… this is all wrong." Kareem lowered his head and lit his cigar.

"Jasmine, history teaches us that anybody can be killed. Who put the price on her head and who took the contract are the answers that we need to know."

"I don't know, Kareem… but I have a better question, where the fuck does this put us? We only have about 400 kilos of cocaine, how long can that hold us over for?"

Jasmine walked up to the bar in her office and took a bottle of Gray Goose out and poured herself a double shot.

"Look Jasmine, I know someone who can turn one kilo into two. Let me make a few calls, but right now we have this meeting to go to in Harlem. And Manhattan tonight, that's what we need to focus on for right now." Jasmine took her double shot down with one gulp.

"Reschedule this meeting, we have bigger problems on our hands now that needs our attention way more than Harlem. We have all the time in the world to kill these motherfuckers, just like we had Nikki Gunz killed okay."

"Okay Jasmine, I'm going to get on that now and reschedule the meeting." Kareem walked off and pulled out his phone to call Drama.

***

"Now Chin, who would have ever saw that coming? Garcia Blanka is dead, murdered at her own house… whoever did that had a point to make."

"Yeah, how you think this is going to play out?"

"Somebody's going to talk, they always do. But what I do know is that cartels kill each other all the time. Mrs. Blanka's number just came up, that's all and someone finally killed her. But before this is over a lot more bodies will fall, I can promise you that Chin," Chin didn't say anything as him and Benny walked out of the junkyard to the limo that was waiting on them.

Chapter 26

The black Maybach pulled up to the pool hall, Drama got out and opened the back door for Nikki to step out. Nikki had a full body hoodie on, all gray as if she was wearing a coat. Mayhem walking next to her with a small box in his hands that was gift wrapped. They walked towards the door to the pool hall and when the doors opened all eyes were on Nikki. Chin got up from the bar and walked over to where Nikki was. He looked at her as if he was looking into a ghost's eyes.

"I thought you was dead?"

"So did a lot of other people... but here I stand, is Benny available?"

"Yes he is, come on I'll show you to him, he's in the back."

"Thank you, Chin."

"No problem, Nikki." Drama and Mayhem followed Chin to the back where Benny was at. When the doors opened Benny had a golf club in his hand, playing golf on a big video game. Benny turned around and looked at Nikki, he placed the golf club down and walked over to her.

"And they say Houdini is the only one who can fake his death, or come back from the dead whoever said that was wrong." Benny walked up to Nikki and gave her a hug.

"I'm glad you are alive, I have to admit I was hurt when I found out you were dead."

"It's going to take more than a Mexican drug lord to stop what I have going on," Benny looked at Nikki funny, then Chin.

"Benny I have something for you, Mayhem... give Benny the box." Benny looked at Mayhem and then took the box from him.

"Come Nikki, let's have a seat at the table while I open this gift up you have for me."

Nikki sat at the table with Benny, Chin watched as Benny opened the box up, once the box was open Benny saw the bloody knife that was in there and he looked back at Nikki.

"I cut that bitch from ear to ear for her role and the attempt on your life as well as mine's Garcia Blanka is a dead bitch." Chin couldn't believe it was Nikki, Nikki reached in her pocket and pulled out her cell phone and showed Benny the picture of Mrs. Blanka dead under the statue. Then there was one more picture, Nikki holding the same knife with the blood dripping off it she had in the box as a gift.

"The knife that I used to slit Garcia Blanka's throat. Benny, I take friendship very personal and she crossed the line and because of that she took her last breath." Benny got up and walked around the table to Nikki. Nikki stood up as Benny kissed her on the forehead.

"Nikki from this day forward you are a friend with us and the pipelines are open. It's at 10% charge now." Nikki looked into Benny's eyes and nodded.

"Thank you, you have my loyalty."

"And you have mine." Nikki walked out the pool hall, once outside Drama looked at her.

"What's next?"

"We have a walking dead bitch to kill, and her nigga too."

***

Chief Ward walked into the briefing room and looked at all the officers and then he said with a loud voice.

"Listen up, listen up… I have the mayor bringing heat down on my ass everyday, there's a damn body count racking up." Chief Ward started smacking the desk as he was screaming to get his point across.

"And the one name that keeps coming up, Nikki Gunz, Nikki Gunz, Nikki Gunz." Captain Fuller stood up.

"Sir, Nikki Gunz is dead as of 2 weeks ago sir." Chief Ward shook his head as he looked at Captain Fuller and smiled.

"Captain, are you sure of that? Did you see a dead body or autopsy report? Did you check the hospital records? Because as of 3 days ago this picture was taken at JFK and guess who the fuck it is… a fucking ghost or Nikki in the flesh, and guess where she came from? I'll wait, Captain."

Captain Fuller sucked his teeth before talking, "Mexico."

"Ding, ding, ding, Captain Fuller just answered the million dollar question. So you know what that means, not only is she taking out bosses here in New York City, but she graduated to killing cartel bosses. This bitch is a fucking problem right now for us, and if she's back in New York after she killed one of the deadliest cartel bosses in history that means somebody's coming up here real soon to see Nikki Gunz and that's what the fuck we don't want. We have to stop this before it starts, crackdown on all her businesses, pull her apes off the streets, the crackdown begins today." "So are we going to need warrants for this? Because the mayor is going to call you for more than just a body count on the streets. Nikki has too many people in her back pocket with too many strong ties."

"So, get the guys off the streets, throw the damn book at them, until someone becomes a fucking rat… do I make myself clear?"

Everybody said, "Yes sir."

"Good, meeting adjourned." Captain Fuller looked at Mac before walking out of the briefing room.

Chapter 27

"Genesis, make this easy on yourself... look at you hanging upside down from the ceiling by chains, you have been getting beat all night, your body is black and blue. Now you can die the easy way or the hard way, it's up to you." Genesis looked at Benzo and spit blood on his shoes then looked up at him. "Fuck you, *puto*." Benzo smiled and snapped his fingers and his two men brought him a bucket of water.

"Let's give her 30 seconds to start off with. Genesis, I hope you can hold your breath." He watched as they placed Genesis' head in the bucket of water as she was hung upside down. He watched as they pulled her out.

"You ready to talk yet?"

"Fuck you, *puto*... kill me, kill me." Genesis said with short breaths, Benzo looked at her then knelt down in front of her.

"No, no... I'm not going to kill you yet. Let me show you who we found last night, I figured we'll bring him to the party." he stood up and gestured to his men.

"Bring the little boy here, let her see who we got." Genesis looked and saw her 8 year old son coming in the shed. When he saw her the first thing he did was yell her name as he tried to run up to her, but they stopped him.

Genesis looked at her son as he was yelling her name.

"Joker, Joker stop crying... it's going to be okay. I need you to be brave for Mommy, Joker," Joker looked at his mom

103

as one of Benzo's men walked into the room with a phone in his hand.

"We found out who it was who killed Mrs. Blanka, it was Nikki. Look Genesis is standing right here with her in the marketplace." Benzo nodded and pulled his gun out.

"Good job Castro, little Joker your mom said be brave so don't cry when you die. Genesis, is there anything you want to say to your son? Matter of fact, just tell him in the afterlife." Benzo pointed the gun at her son and pulled the trigger, shooting him in the chest and killing him instantly. Genesis yelled when she saw her son's body slumped to the floor. Benzo walked over to her and pointed the gun at her head and shot her twice, killing her. He then looked at his men,

"Guys, feed their bodies to the pigs… they are scum, but keep their heads. I have a use for them." Benzo said as he walked off.

***

"Drama, oh shit, it's time to jump out, their boys they hitting the block. Come on we have to get the fuck out of here," Drama looked at the police trolling the block, he took off running with Mayhem as they had four officers running behind them. They were in between two buildings jumping a gate as Mayhem looked back and saw the two officers were right behind them still. Drama jumped on a garbage dumpster and climbed the ladder. Mayhem was right behind him, it wasn't until they were both on the roof that Drama stopped to catch his breath. Mayhem ran next to him, "Yo, this shit is crazy, we have lost 2 kilos on the streets. Nikki is going to be 38 hot about this one." "Who the fuck are you telling this shit to? Somebody's going to die because of this shit," before Drama could say another word both officers were on the roof looking at them. Drama looked at Mayhem and both of them took off running to the edge of the building and jumped across to the other building. The officers looked at each other and shook their heads as Mayham and Drama stuck their middle fingers up at the officers laughing as they walked off.

***

Captain Fuller walked over to the cell and looked at all 15 guys they pulled off the streets. Chief Ward walked up to him, "We have one kilo and 10 guns, someone is going to talk now… it's up to you to find out who, Captain."

"I'll get on that right now, sir."

"Good, you see the one with the gray hoodie on? Talk to him first, he was the one with kilo in the book bag. I know he has something to say." Chief Ward walked off, leaving Captain Fuller standing there looking at the man in the hoodie.

Chapter 28

"Did you see Captain Fuller, out there Mayhem?"

"No, there was only 20 or more blue and whites. Shit was crazy, they booked about 20 of our guys, but I have Remy going down there getting them out now. Buckshot got knocked up with the kilo and nobody saw this shit coming." Nikki, motherfuckers jumped out of a U-Haul truck with their guns out like it was a hit". Nikki pulled her phone out and called Captain Fuller, after a few rings he picked up.

"Hold on, let me lock my office door." Captain Fuller locked his office door and then sat behind his desk.

"Nikki, what the fuck? I thought you were dead, I went to your funeral and all. "

"A lot of people thought I was dead, but I'm very much alive."

"I see that now."

"Let's cut the bullshit, why are your officers running down on my men?"

"That was out of my hands, Nikki."

"Then you need to find a way to get it back in your fucking hands before you go back on the fucking boat ride."

"Is that a threat Nikki?"

"No, it's a fucking promise… threat's are for kids, I'm a grown ass bitch, I make promises. Nigga now get your hands back on this case." Nikki hung up the phone and looked at Drama.

"Get the apes back on the block, we are losing money... how much money was given for my services?"

"All together it was $450,000."

"Good, get two food trucks we are feeding Harlem tonight. Matter of fact I want to throw a big ass fair, we are going to show Harlem some love like they have never seen before."

"Cool, I'll get on that now."

Just as Drama was getting up to leave Mayhem came walking in the door with a box in his hand, Nikki looked at him as Mayhem placed the box on the table.

"Where did that come from Mayhem?"

"The mailman just dropped it off."

Nikki got up from the desk and walked around to the table she seen the postmark on the box that said Mexico, in her heart she already knew what was in the box. She took her knife out and cut the box open, and just like she thought it was Genesis' head along with her son's. She closed her eyes and closed the box up.

"Drama, take this to the funeral home and have Mr. Carmen cremate them and put them into urns with their names on it."

"What's the names?"

"Have him put in loving memory of Genesis and Joker." Drama picked up the box.

"Okay, I'm going to do that now."

"Thank you."

As Drama left the room with Mayhem, a Mariah Carey song came on the radio, *My All*, and for the first time in many years she thought about Malachi and the day she kissed him. She hated Malachi for making her into a monster, but just like Malachi, Mrs. Blanka, Cruise and everyone else she killed she knew her time was coming, and Genesis' head was a sign that they were coming to kill her. She was going to face them head on, this was the life she lived and she feared no one, and the only way she was going to leave it was death. That was the only way she was going to sign out of this life.

Chapter 29

"So, this is where you be at 4 Tray?"

4 Tray pulled on the blunt and passed it to Tasha before talking. "Yeah, little Mama, this is the block and this is my team. We call it the danger zone, facts."

"I hear you Mr. I'm at the Danger Zone, facts." 4 Tray couldn't help but to like Tasha. She was dark skin with a Coca-Cola body, brilliant white smile. He loved the fact she could dress her ass off, he invited her to the danger zone to a kickback they were having there. They had music playing, some Lil Baby and you had people rolling dice, playing cards, talking shit to each other, that's when Tasha look and saw Kidd smoking a blunt with a few of the guys a few feet away from her.

"I thought you said y'all don't fuck with the apes and Harlem?"

"We don't fuck with them dudes at all, hands down...our orders are to smoke on sight, facts." Tasha looked at him and rolled her eyes.

"What the fuck is all that about?" 4 Tray said as he was grilling Tasha.

"It can't be all smoke on sight because that nigga over there with the black hoodie on, he's one of Nikki's apes, and that's a fact." 4 Tray looked over at Kidd, "are you sure?"

"Yeah, I've been seeing him in Harlem with all the rest of them niggas. Mayhem said him and Drama used to be at Ruckus Park all the time... matter of fact, hold on." Tasha pulled out her phone and showed 4 Tray pictures of Kidd on her homegirl's IG page with some of Nikki apes. 4 Tray gritted his teeth in a state of rage.

"That pussy motherfucker. Good looking out beautiful, on the heads up. Check it out, send me that picture to my phone."

"I got you," 4 Tray looked at Kidd as he was joking and smoking a blunt with other niggas around him not knowing his clock just started ticking.

***

Jasmine was holding a kilo of cocaine in her hands as she looked at the table stacked with cocaine. She placed the kilo back down on the table and walked over to Kareem.

"Kareem, how many kilos are on the table?"

"150, I had 75 kilos turned into 150 kilos… and that still leaves us with 250 untouched kilos."

"Good, don't touch them. But the question remains, I want to know is how is the quality of it?"

"I knew you was going to ask me that, it's 70% pure… each one of them." Jasmine shook her head, "So when are we going to put them on the streets?" "I already have 4 Tray and Youngin with a few men teaming up and hugging the block right now, getting the money."

"Good now that is taken care of let's set this meeting up with them cats from Harlem, we need to branch out more now."

"I'm already on that, I set the meeting up this week, same place."

"Sounds good," Jasmine said as she walked to Kareem and kissed him on the forehead before leaving.

***

"Nigga, you're over here looking 38 hot, like Tasha's pussy wasn't talking about shit."

"Real talk homie, I fucked up big time..." Youngin looked at 4 Tray sideways.

"What you talking about?"

"That nigga Kidd, he ain't right at all."

"What the fuck you mean by that? Stop talking to me in circles, nigga."

4 Tray looked at Youngin and shook his head.

"He'a a fucking rat, he's one of Nikki's boys."

"Man, get the fuck out of here, that's crazy!"

"No, dead ass. Tasha pointed that nigga out to me tonight bro."

"You can't take the word of no bitch, Tasha just talking... you know bitches be full of talking just so she can suck a nigga dick. She knows you are getting that cake, now you can't go off no bitch word bro." 4 Tray handed his phone to Youngin, showing him the picture she sent him.

"Yo, this shit is bananas... this nigga really has been a fucking rat the whole time. Now all this shit is getting put together."

"Dead ass, I'mma have to body this nigga and tell Kareem some crazy shit because I put my stamp on him, that means this shit fall back on me. That means I'm going to stop this nigga from breathing, before Kareem stops me from breathing."

"Yo fuck that nigga, we going to roast his ass tomorrow night... we will make it look like a play that went bad."

"Thanks, good looking out. That's loyalty and love, fam."

"You already know you are my dog from the sandbox to the grave, you know how we fucking rock." 4 Tray dapped Youngin up as they smoked the blunt in the car, looking at Kidd.

Chapter 30

"Look man, I don't fucking talk to your kind… so fuck off, you get what the fuck I'm saying?"

"So you think you are a tough guy? You might have heart in the streets, you may even have a few guys that are scared of you… but I ain't none of them motherfuckers at all, you get me?"

"Like I said, I don't have nothing to say fuck you." "You don't have nothing to say about shit, but you will listen to what the fuck I got to say. You got caught with a kilo of cocaine and a loaded 45 caliber, you are looking at 25 years right now. I could drop the gun charge, that's 5 years off the table and I'll talk to the DA about your cooperation and get that 20 down to 10. You might even get out in 6 years, give or take." Buckshot looked at Detective Kent with a smile on his face. "Let me put it to you this way, Detective. You can suck my dick, I ain't no fucking rat I'm going to take my 25 years and put it on my chest, cop." Detective Kent knocked twice on the table and smiled. "See you in 25 years, buddy." Buckshot just watched as Detective Kent walked out of the interrogation room.

***

4 Tray walked to Kidd as he was leaning against the building smoking a blunt making a play.

"Yo, what's the word 4 Tray?"

"I need you to take a ride with me and Youngin on a drop off real quick."

"Sayless fam, let's ride out."

"Come on, Youngin in waiting on us now." Kidd walked off, following 4 Tray over to Youngin's car.

"So where we riding out to?" 4 Tray got in the front seat of the car.

"We're headed to Southside Jamaica Queens, to drop these two kilos off for Kareem real quick. Then we are headed to the warehouse to drop the money off." "That's the business then." Youngin started blasting the music in the car as 4 Tray pulled the gun out and cocked it back. Kidd was texting on his phone and not paying attention, 4 Tray turned around real quick with his gun in his hand and started shooting Kidd in the chest, killing him. Youngin pulled over a few blocks down and they pulled Kidd out of the car and flopped his body next to a garbage dumpster. 4 Tray and Youngin got back in the car as Youngin pulled off.

"Yo, you put the coke on him right?"

"Fucking right, and I dropped the quarter bird on that nigga just so the police will think it was a robbery going bad and Jasmine and them could think it was a setup, like he got hit."

"Real shit, smart thinking… now come on, let's drop this fucking hot box off… this car is on fire right now."

Chapter 31

Nikki sat at her desk with her phone, she looked at the unknown number and picked it up. "Hello?" and a deep Mexican accent someone said, "I was seeing if you received the package I sent you?" Nikki looked out at her shop at the two armed apes. "Why did you send me that gift?" "Because it's two gifts you left behind, and my beautiful country in Mexico at a very dear friend of mine's house. I think you know what I mean…"

"I do, but after they came to see me first I'll take that very personal, so I did it myself. My only regret is I only got to kill that *puto* one fucking time. But I enjoyed cutting that throat from ear to ear, now the only question is how long do you have to live? Because if you come at me, I promise you my face will be the last face you see before you see God." "Nikki, I will see you soon.. I just need you to remember one thing, and that's I'm not Garcia Blanka." "That's a good thing, because when I slit your throat I'm not just going to walk away. I'm going to stand there and watch you bleed out as you try to catch your breath and before you die my face is going to be the last thing you fucking see." With that Nikki hung up the phone and thought about her next move.

***

"We been investigating Stacy Hall, AKA Nikki Gunz for the last 6 years. She's been able to get through every crack we laid out for her. Not only that, she has taken out cartel bosses, mob bosses, Malachi Williams, let's face the fact… she's a deadly bitch. But we can use her, Senior Director Cockright, we just got word that she recently had a meeting with Benny and the Italian mob. And that's big gentlemen, I think it's time we made her a deal that she can't refuse." FBI Agent Marcus said looking around at everyone in the room, Director Cockright looked around before speaking.

"Agent Marcus, you bring up a good point, there are a lot of bad guys that Nikki can have conversations with that can come out every time in our favor. What I can say about Nikki is when the kitchen is too hot for everyone else, it's just right for her, but remember we are not the CIA we can't do what they do at all."

"Sir, all we have to do is show her we can and will protect her. We can have her do our dirty work, every mob boss, cartel boss and street gang did what I'm suggesting right now." Senior Director Cockright looked at Agent Marcus.

"Okay, let's play your game since you have a strong feeling about this. Since you claim she would be an asset if you get her to sign up with us, Agent Marcus."

"I'll get on it right now sir."

"Good, let me know something as soon as possible."

Everyone got up and walked out the room, suddenly Senior Director Cockright called Agent Marcus "Marcus, hold on a minute." Marcus walked over to the Director.

"Yes sir?"

"Don't let this blow up in your face because your ass is on the line right now."

"I understand sir."

"Good, now go make this happen for us."

"Yes sir," Agent Marcus walked out the room as Director Cockright patted him on the back.

Chapter 32

"Yo Kareem, I need to holler at you for a second, boss."

Kareem turned around and looked at 4 Tray as he walked up to him.

"What's up?"

"Last night Kidd got rolled, they got a half a bird off him."

"Where they catch him slipping at?"

" Flatbush, already trying to find out who did it and let me know."

"4 Tray, I understand shit happens… but you still owe $15,000 because he was your stamp, so that's your debt now."

"Sayless bro, I'll take care of it."

***

"Nikki you have an Agent Marcus downstairs to see you." Nicki looked at the camera screen in her office.

"Bring him up, let's see what FBI Agent Marcus has to say."

"I'll do that now," Nikki walked over to her bar and got two glasses and a bottle of Ciroc and placed it on the table just as there was a knock at the door. She walked over and opened it and looked at Drama and Agent Marcus.

"Drama, I can take it from here. Agent Marcus, please come in and have a seat."

"Thank you Nikki." Nikki closed the door as she walked to the table and poured them a drink she passed Agent Marcus his glass as she sat across from him.

"So, Agent Marcus… tell me what can I do for you? To what do I owe the pleasure of this visit? You're by yourself so I know it's not official that's why I offered you a drink." Agent Marcus let out a laugh as he took another sip of his Ciroc and set the glass down on the table.

"Nikki, you are good at what you do. I can't lie, we know that you had Malachi killed, along with Garcia Blanka and many others. We can use someone of your unique skill set." Nikki picked up her glass and she took a sip of her drink before responding,

"I would never even think or talk to you about this, are you serious Agent Marcus?"

"Nikki, I'm deadly serious, because I'm the one who can save your life and get you everything you need to stay in operation…guns, drugs, protection from the law."

"I'm not a rat at all, I don't cooperate with authorities, I'm not good at that." Agent Marcus smiled and took another sip of his drink, "We are not asking you to be a rat at all, we wouldn't disrespect what you've built like that. Let me show you something." Agent Marcus pulled out a folder with pictures inside of it along with a small video camera. He passed everything to Nikki. Nikki looked at the pictures of her and Garcia Blanka, showing how she killed Malachi and then she pressed play on the video camera and was looking at herself as she shot Malachi several times after having a conversation.

"Yeah, we know you killed him. Oldham had to send this to the FBI Senior Director Cockright. Oldham was smart, he had everything in place just in case anything ever happened to him. This alone gives you the death sentence, so I think you might want to play ball with us. Look at it this way, it's a win-win for the both of us, plus I'll pull some strings and get your guys out the big house." Nikki placed the file down on her desk.

"How do I know I can trust you? After all, you and Captain Fuller have been trying to get me for years." "Let me put it to you this way Nikki, you're not in cuffs…so that should say a lot."

"Here's my counteroffer, get my guys from behind bars then come back and talk to me. I had one of my female apes go down there to bond them out, but they turned around at the door. Do that for me and show me you are for real." Agent Marcus took his last sip of Ciroc and knocked on the table twice before standing to leave.

"I'll be in touch Nikki." he said before walking out of her office.

The FBI played their game all too well, but for the loyalty to her apes she knew she'd make the choice he wanted her to make. In order to save them she would make a deal with the devil even if she had to sign her name and blood on the dotted line.

Chapter 33

Drama was smoking a blunt riding around Harlem when he pulled up on Sid posted up on the block, he stepped out of the car and walked up to him and dapped him up.

"What's the word Sid?"

"Shit hurt son, looking at Kidd in that wooden box, dog."

"I already know, Nikki ain't going to let this shit fly, that I promise you... that's on apes because I know 4 Tray and Youngin are behind this bullshit, facts."

"Check me out, Nikki is about to roll these niggas. Nikki ain't letting shit ride, trust and believe that homie." Drama passed Sid the blunt.

"Sayless let's me know is all I ask. When you ride on these niggas come get me, this shit is personal."

"I swear on the Blood Diamond Cartel, we got you." Drama dapped Sid up and got back in the car and pulled off.

***

It was 8pm, Jasmine looked at Kareem when she got into the black SUV.

"You ready for this Kareem?"

"Yeah, we have two cars coming with us and everyone is fully loaded. We are meeting Mayham and Drama at the park." "Good, and if something don't feel right shoot everything."

"That's already understood," Jasmine didn't say another word and she sat quietly in the SUV as they rode to the park.

***

Nikki checked both of her guns as she looked at Drama just as they were about to pull out.

"We pull up you and Mayhem get out of the car first, when Jasmine starts talking, hear what she has to say before you come over to my door and let me out. Let them believe that they got the rope around our necks, then make sure everyone is ready because if we have to throw down, shit is going to go boom."

"We already know, we got everybody ready, cocked and locked. If she gets out of hand we are going to body these motherfuckers, hands down."

"Believe me, I already know where your loyalty is at." Nikki walked to the black BMW door, Mayhem opened the door for her and she turned and looked around at all her apes ready to ride out, they was four cars deep.

***

Jasmine stayed quiet in in the backseat of the truck as Kareem, 4 Tray and Youngin were in the front of the truck with a few guys surrounding them. Everyone had their guns in their hands watching as the BMW and Mercedes were pulling up with two SUVs behind them. Kareem watched as Drama stepped out the BMW with his gun in his hand, so did Mayhem. They stepped in front of the cars, at the same time Youngin walked up to the back of the truck and opened the door for Jasmine to step out, she walked next to Kareem and looked at everyone.

"Drama, let me get to the point… Nikki is dead, and I have enough product to supply Harlem so you and your crew can continue to eat. I'm thinking a 70/30 split, nobody wants to go to war but I will take it there if I have to." Drama looked around at all the guys Jasmine had around her with their guns in their hands.

"Jasmine, that's your name right? You said a 70/30 split, that's funny as hell... then you mentioned war like we are scared to die. Nikki had us stepping like the mob, we all know death comes with this life. See Jasmine, you never raised apes and you never were a gorilla. You never was bred like a gorilla. See, Malachi knew how to make a monster... you and Kareem brought your loyalty from these niggas you got around y'all, but these niggas behind me? Nicki bred her apes with loyalty and trust. She knew how to kill without a heart, but I'm not at liberty to have this conversation with you. So, if you don't mind hold on one second... somebody else wants to have this conversation with you." Jasmine looked at Kareem wondering what was going on, they watched as Mayhem walked to the back of the BMW and opened the door everyone watched as Nicki got out the car and walked up to Drama like the boss bitch she was. Jasmine and Kareem looked at Nikki as she had her gun in her hand standing next to Drama.

"Jasmine and Kareem, you two look like you saw a ghost... wait, you two thought I was dead? It's going to take more than a sniper to kill me, but hey like I always say, my shooters don't miss. It's when you come at me that I take that fucking personal, so just like Hardbody I walked up to him and shot him in the fucking face, and just like Garcia Blanka I slit her fucking throat from ear to ear." Jasmine looked at Kareem and then back at Nikki with hate in her eyes. "So let me tell you a little story, Mrs. Blanka had me come to Mexico, she needed me to do what you and Malachi couldn't Jasmine, and that was kill Senor Cruise. So I dressed up like a call girl and when I got him alone, I stabbed him so many times that when I was done it was like I took a blood bath, it was like something out of a horror movie. Then I cut his fucking heart out of his chest. For that act of loyalty, Mrs.

Blanka gave me my girls and showed me how to move like the cartel, to kill how, how to be an apex predator. I spent 3 weeks down there training with her and then I called her one night and told her how I felt about Malachi and she told me he was weak-hearted, he wasn't strong enough to run the cartel. So she gave me an offer that I couldn't refuse..." Jasmine reached behind her back holding her gun as Nikki was talking, Kareem and Drama maintained eye contact, tension was thick in the air and everyone felt it.

"She told me that if I was to kill Malachi she would supply me with all the cocaine I needed, plus a bonus, I can run my own cartel. So I went to the farm where I knew Malachi would be at, and just like I thought, he was standing there looking out the window smoking a cigar. The look on his face was priceless when he saw Mrs. Blanka walk through the doors, what was even more priceless was when he saw me pointing a gun at his fucking face. He actually turned around and looked at me, he was shocked. I told him he was retarded, he looked at Garcia Blanka then back at me and said "Where do we go from here?" and I said "you are going to a fucking grave *puto* you fucking son of a bitch." it was funny because I blew his fucking brains out the back of his head, afterwards I stood over him and I shot his ass some more..." when Jasmine heard that she pulled the gun from behind her back and started shooting at Nikki, Drama, and Mayhem were shooting at Kareem. Bullets were flying, there were members from both sides ducking down behind the cars and trucks that were getting shot up.

"Nikki, I swear you are a dead bitch... I'm going to fucking kill you." Jasmine said as she came out from behind the car shooting at Nikki. Nikki had ducked down behind the car.

"You tried that already and I'm still here." Nikki heard Jasmine's gun clip empty as she came from behind the car and looked at Jasmine she pointed her gun at her.

"Bye bitch, give Malachi my regards." as Nikki fired the gun, 4 Tray jumped in front of the bullet, preventing Jasmine from getting hit. Nikki looked around she had two apes on the ground and Jasmine had two dead bodies everybody was still shooting.

"Nikki, we got to get the fuck out of here now! The police is coming!"

"Get them two apes in the car, we're not going nowhere without them." Mayhem and someone else got the two apes in the car as Jasmine and Kareem got in the trucks, everyone pulling out before the police came. Jasmine was holding 4 Tray's hand looking dead at him, as Kareem was driving out of there.

"4 Tray, fight... don't die on me, fight this." 4 Tray looked at Jasmine one last time before taking his last breath. Jasmine took her hand and closed his eyes, knowing he was dead...and she was left holding a lifeless body.

Chapter 34

"You have to be fucking kidding me? Are you fucking for real?" Chief Ward cursed, reading over the release papers that Agent Marcus gave to him. "Chief Ward, I know the manhours you put in to get these guys off the streets, but this is above my head... you know how bad we all want to see Nikki behind bars."

"Marcus I hear you, but this is some fucking bullshit, me and you both know it." Chief Ward cut his eyes to the window to his office as some of Nikki's apes were walking past the window sticking their middle fingers up at him and laughing as they were been escorted out of the precinct. Chief Ward looked at Agent Marcus.

"You tell your boss he just let murderers, drug dealers, and a whole bunch of other deviants we spent countless manhours getting behind bars and they are walking out the fucking precinct with a get out of jail free card. So next time the news come on and they are talking about the murders in Harlem, people being kidnapped, you tell Senior Director Cockright their blood is on his hands." Chief Ward pinned Agent Marcus with his gaze.

"The door is that way, maybe you can show them the way to freedom." Agent Marcus smiled and walked out of the office not saying a word.

***

Jasmine was yelling at the top of her lungs as she looked at everyone around her, "I was told this bitch was fucking dead by you Youngin and 4 Tray died in my fucking arms. Then this bitch told me to my fucking face that she killed Malachi. I want her fucking dead, do you fucking hear me?" Jasmine looked at Youngin as she walked up to him, Kareem just watched.

"Youngin, you told me she was fucking dead... do you know what that looks like? You have any clue what the fuck just happened out there, because you didn't know what the fuck a dead bitch look like?"

"Jasmine, we all thought she was dead from the way that bullet hit her."

"I look like a fucking fool last night, look at me here... what the fuck am I saying very fucking clearly. This will be the last time you hear me say this shit." Youngin just looked at Jasmine as she pulled her gun out and pointed at his face with everybody watching.

"You pull your gun out, you point your gun at the motherfucker you want to kill, and then you pull the trigger like this." All they could hear was the echo of the gunshot as Jasmine pulled the trigger. All they saw was Youngin and blood being splatted all over the wall. His body hit the floor and Jasmine stood over his body and shot him until her gum was completely empty. She didn't look at anybody else in the room.

"Every fucking body in this room, that's how you kill a motherfucker. You see this nigga, this is what dead looks like. I don't want to have this conversation again, next time somebody else is going to be laying on the fucking floor. Now get the fuck out my face."

***

Nikki walked down the stairs from her office to the main floor as everyone looked at her.

"We live, we fucking die. We all know what we signed up for but I ride out from all my apes 20 of y'all were just behind bars not even 48 hours ago each of you looking at 25 years plus, but here you are, free of all charges, everything dropped because how you ride for me I ride for you. In the streets and behind closed doors, I would never ask you how to do something I wouldn't do. I killed Hardbody and Malachi, I killed Garcia Blanka...some may ask why? Because when someone fucks with you, they fuck with me. You put your life on the line for me, I put my life on the line for you. You die for me, and I'll die for you. We are the strongest cartel in the States. Last night we pulled up and showed out, I'm throwing a fair for Harlem I want everyone to be on point... there will be kids out there and not one of them better get hurt. Drama, Mayhem, put everybody where they need to be."

"We're on it Nikki."

"And to my fallen apes, I want everything tiptop for their funerals and send their mothers $400,000 a piece, we take care of ours dead or alive."

Chapter 35

"Handrus, when are we going to see about Nikki?" Handrus sat at the bench peeling the apple with his knife as he looked at the lake in the backyard. "Mecca, Nikki is very smart... she has a lot of strings and connections. She is waiting on us to strike, she learned a lot from Mrs. Blanka she is very patient, if we strike now she will be waiting for us. So we wait patiently, she's at war with Jasmine and Kareem, let her think the war is over and when she's at home thinking she has peace for the night I will send 20 killers to her front door and they will have her dead body laying in a pool of blood dead. I might even be the one to pull the trigger to take her life." Mecca nodded before walking off leaving Handrus in peace eating his apple looking at the sun over the lake in peace.

***

Captain Fuller walked around the fair smoking a cigar looking at all the children laughing and eating cotton candy when Chief Ward walked up behind him.

"You have to be fucking kidding me? What she's a fucking fairy godmother now?"

"Every child needs one, even the ones in Harlem Chief."

"Yeah, what is she going to do? Teach them how to kill, sell drugs, throw people of the top of rooftop buildings like Mason in the supreme team. This fair food, rides, and games is all some sort of bullshit. Mark my word Fuller, mark my fucking words." Captain Fuller and Chief Ward stopped talking when they caught sight of Nikki taking pictures with the kids, smiling and making funny faces as the children walked up. Drama tapped Nikki on the shoulder and pointed towards Captain Fuller and Chief Ward. Nikki smiled and walked towards both of them with Drama beside her.

"Chief Ward, Captain Fuller, I'm glad you were able to make it to the fair. Everything is free here, the food, rides, games, can I get the two of you something to eat? I know New York finest are often hungry."

" I already ate so I will have to respectfully decline," Nikki smiled as she looked at Chief Ward, "and what about you, Captain?"

"No thanks, Nikki. I greatly appreciate your offer but I ate already as well."

"Well, please enjoy yourselves, as you can see I have other guests to attend to. Have a nice day gentlemen." Nikki smiled and walked off.

"Drama, find that video tape of me and Captain Fuller eating on the boat and send a copy of that tape to him, just to make sure he knows who he is playing with. Sometimes when you let a dog off the chain you have to remind them he can always get put back on that chain. Also, have someone kill Kareem… it's time we strike first."

"I'll do that, because this is personal."

"Just get it done."

***

"So I think it's safe to say Nikki bit the poison apple she agreed to do what we asked, as long as it doesn't have anything to do with ratting. But whoever we need for her to take out she's game." Senior Director Cockright took a sip of his coffee."I see, so what does she want in return?"

"Instead of supplying the cocaine since she already has the connect, she just needs a safe route for her supply that's all."

"We will give her what she is asking for, did her guys get released?"

"Every one of them."

"What did that fat fuck say to you as they walked out the station? How did he take that?"

"With a red face, and he told me to tell you when the murderers and drug dealers and kidnappers start the innocent blood is on your hands."

"What the fuck ever. I never liked that fat fuck anyway, not yesterday, today, or tomorrow... Nikki is going to run New York and we are going to run Nikki. That's just the way the cookie crumbles."

"Yep, that's the way the cookie crumbles." Agent Marcus said with a small smile on his face.

Chapter 36

"Y'all come on, we need to make these drop offs now and two pickups before the night gets away from us." Drama watched as he put his hoodie on he had two Mac 11's with him with extended 100 round clip ready for action. He put the murder one mask over his face he started creeping from the side of the SUV.

"Yo, Sea-Town, make sure you get that bag on the back side too with them two other bags. Load them up man, yo Killer, you in the front with me." Kareem walk to the front of the truck looking down at his phone Drama ran up on him and yelled.

"Yo, Kareem... Nikki said what up, pussy." Kareem looked and saw the Mac 11 pointed dead at his ass, he dropped his phone as sparks from the Mac 11 were flying his way. Bullet casings were dropping. Kareem was hit in the chest and arms, Killer ran from the side of the truck and went to shoot at Drama but his gun jammed. Drama pointed the Mac 11 at Killer as he started to run back, but he got hit in the back from the Mac 11. Drama ran up to Killer and sprayed 20 rounds into him, he then walked over to Kareem and looked down at him. Kareem looked up as he was holding his chest.

"Fuck nigga, you thought this shit was sweet... you thought she was dead. Nikki ain't dead motherfucker, but you are about to be." Just as Drama was about to pull the trigger,

Sea-Town came from the side of the SUV with the Mossburg pump.

"Time to die, Kareem."

"Yeah, but it's your time to die motherfucker." Drama looked at Sea-Town holding the Mossburg. Sea-Town pulled the trigger letting the double round hit Drama's chest, blowing him back. Sea-Town picked Kareem up and helped him in the truck. He looked back at Drama laying still on the ground as he jumped in the driver seat and pulled off. Drama saw a blur as the truck pulled away. He held his chest, taking short breaths the bulletproof vest he had on stopped the rounds from putting a hole in his chest. He got back in the SUV and pulled off holding his chest.

Chapter 37

Captain Fuller watched the video tape of him and Nikki eating on her boat. He couldn't believe she had in full. He didn't know what he was thinking, even down to the part where he took the money... she had everything on tape. Attached to the tape there was a note that said *call me, you have 24 hours.* It was 7:00 pm he picked up the phone and called Nikki after a few rings she picked up as she was riding in the back seat of her Maybach headed to a meeting.

"Captain, I see you received the package I had sent you."

"Nikki, what do you want from me? Everything you asked of me to do I did already...so what more do you want from me?"

"Captain, me and you have been playing cat and mouse for years now... what you need to know is that I'm always going to win. I'm always going to be two steps ahead of you, I could have killed you a hundred times already...so let me put this to you this way, in this life we live I'm God to you, motherfucker. Next time I offer you something to eat, you say yes. If I offered you something to drink, you say please and thank you."

"My chief was there, Nikki... what was I supposed to do?" Nikki smiled.

"I don't give a fuck if the governor was there talking to the president and the Pope. You say yes please, and thank you. Do I make myself clear?" Captain Fuller bit down on his lip trying to keep from lashing out and telling her what he really thought. He honestly hated Nikki with his whole heart.

"Yes, as clear as water."

"Good, because I would hate to have to cut your head off with a sword just to show a motherfucker don't play with it. Now you have a good night, I have a meeting I'm about to attend." Nikki hung up the phone as her car pulled into the garage. The door was opened up as a car pulled in, her driver walked around the car to her door and opened it for her. She glanced around the surroundings as she walked up to Agent Marcus.

"Agent Marcus, what is this place?"

"Some people call it Hell, others Paradise... come follow me, what we have for you is over here Nikki." She followed him through the warehouse looking at all the kilos of cocaine stacked up to the ceiling, she walked past tables and tables of cocaine until she reached the table where they had 400 kilos on it.

"This is for you, 400 kilos of pure cocaine. 100% pure, this is a gift from my boss to you," Nikki walked over to the table and picked up a kilo and looked at it, then turned around and looked at Agent Marcus, "You said this is a gift, don't nothing come free in my business... in return, what does your boss want?"

"Blood in the streets, the mayor is up for reelection he needs to show New York City that he is not the man for the job. So, here's the deal... 400 kilos for blood in the streets. Look at it this way, you will be taking over new blocks and turfs and with the new supply of powder we are giving you, you would never have to worry about a dry spell." Nikki nodded.

"Let me make this clear, we will eat on when and where we choose. But I promise you this you will have your blood in the streets."

"That's all we ask Nikki, you have yourself a deal. Hey, you two, load this up for her and put it in her car now." Nikki looked around, she knew she was playing with fire but it wasn't like she never was burned before... she knew when it came down to it, it was always shoot to get shot, period.

***

"Sea-Town what the fuck happened?" Jasmine asked him as she looked at Kareem in the room getting worked on from the private doctor?

"I don't know what happened, all I know is shit popped off real fast and went 0 to 100. All I remember was Kareem asking me to put the bags in the back of the SUV then I heard someone say his name, and then that Nikki said what's up pussy... then bullets were flying and shells were dropping. Killer's shit jammed on him, shit was ugly as fuck... I saw the bro take his last breath as he hit the ground. I had the pump in my hand so I saw the nigga with the mask on about to end Kareem's career. I came from the back of the truck and put the rounds in his chest and got Kareem off the ground and in the truck and we took off. Dude was bleeding out bad." "You did the right thing Sea-Town you were thinking fast, I just want to know how did Nikki know where the fuck that location was?" Jasmine stopped talking when the doctor came out the room she watched as he took his bloody gloves off.

"How is he doctor?"

"He was hit pretty bad, shot five times... he's very lucky to be alive. If you would have got here an hour later he would be in a black bag. He needs to recover for the next few weeks, he should be up and running again I'm not going to say at 100%, but let's push for a 65 /70% it's going to take a lot of time for his body to heal properly."

"Thank you, doctor. I really appreciate you coming down and here you go." Jasmine passed him a white envelope with $50,000 inside of it, he took the envelope and walked out.

"Sea-Town don't move, you are here for now. I will send two more guys by here to help guard him with you, I'm sending the nurse by too." "Sayless, I'm posted up." Jasmine didn't say anything else as she walked out the door thinking how the fuck did Nikki know about the warehouse in order to send her shooters there?

***

Nikki stepped out of her car at the auto parts shop and looked at Mayhem before she called him over to her.

"Take out all the kilos in the trunk and place them in stacks of 10 over there on the table... where is Drama at?"

"He's in the back, he got hit in the chest with the pump... lucky he had a vest on."

"Okay, I'm going to see about him now... make sure everything is in stacks of 10."

"Will do." Mayhem called two more guys over to help him unload the trunk of the car. Nikki walk to the back room where Drama was laying down on the couch with a ice pack over his chest. She walked over to the medicine cabinet and got some Icy Hot cream and walked over to where Drama was at. She sat next to him on the couch she took her hand and placed the cream on his chest and was rubbing it in for him.

"Drama, what happened out there last night?" with a low tone Drama said.

"I pulled up on Kareem and they were running three deep. I put the murder one mask over my face and I crept up on him and said, "Yo, Nikki said what's up pussy," then I clapped his ass then some other nigga ran up and I bodied him too... another nigga came out of nowhere I forgot he was even there with the pump, and he hit me in the chest and pushed my shit back. I think he thought I was dead because he didn't even come check to see if I was alive, he didn't do no head shot. All I saw was a blur of the black SUV pulling off." Nikki took the can and place it down on the table.

"Why did you go by yourself? You should have brought Mayhem or someone else with you."

"Nikki, that shit was personal... when he shot at you I promised I was going to kill his ass period. I'm just glad Kidd told me about that whorehouse before he was killed. That's how I knew where he was going to be at." For the first time in a long time Nicki looked at a man as a man, she closed her eyes and lowered her head and kissed Drama on the lips, followed by her tongue touching his. Nikki stood up and walked to the door and locked it. She walked back to Drama as he stood up in front of her and watch her get undressed. As she pulled her shirt off displaying her hourglass figure, Drama was lost for words. As he watched her slowly getting undressed she pulled her pants down and looked at him, as he took his pants off his boxers had a print of his manhood pressed against them. Nikki looked at him as she sat down on the couch she grabbed his hand and pulled him down and looked in his eyes.

"Drama, I haven't been with a man since I was forced to by Malachi. That's been over 8 years ago, it's hard for me to lay with someone in that way again. Please don't make me regret this, I do love you but I know love will get you killed." Drama leaned over and kissed Nikki lips.

"I would never hurt you, I love you today, tomorrow, and always. I will never hurt you, never the only way I would hurt you is by sacrificing my life to save yours. And knowing you can never look at me again, never hear my voice again, never touch my hand again." Nikki felt her heartbreaking, she hadn't heard words like that come out of a man's mouth for so long. Drama leaned forward and kissed her as he held her down on the couch. She looked in his eyes as he placed himself inside of her, she let out a loud moan as her nails were digging into his back as he started moving his hips in circular motion. The sensation was a feeling that Nikki hadn't had in a very long time. Just the feeling of his manhood as he slid in and out of her made her climax harder than she ever had. Drama was giving her deep strokes as Nikki closed her eyes and had her legs wrapped around his back.

"Drama, I need you to slide out some, I can feel you in my stomach." Drama took his lips and covered her mouth and paid her no mind he went deeper inside of her. Nikki dug her nails harder into his back as she looked into his eyes, she felt Drama's seeds being released inside of her.

Chapter 38

Jasmine was riding down 122nd and Park when her car was pulled over, her driver pulled over to the side of the road.

"Jasmine, its Captain Fuller and he looks to be by himself."

"Good, let's see what this fat fuck wants." Captain Fuller walked up to the back window and knocked twice, Jasmine rolled the window down and looked at him.

"Captain, what do I owe the pleasure of this traffic stop?"

"Jasmine, step out of the car please. I need to have a word with you now." Jasmine took her glasses off as she stepped out of the car and walked with Captain Fuller back to his car.

"What do you want Captain? I'm a very busy woman."

"We both have a problem, one that's getting on both our fucking nerves and that's a pain in my ass and I know yours too." Jasmine nodded and smiled.

"Let me guess, Nikki?"

"Yeah… Nikki."

"So I'll listen, you pulled me over for a reason… what's on your mind Captain?"

"I want you to kill this bitch, I'm going to set it up for you… just don't miss."

"The only thing you have to do is tell me the time and day, I will be there personally to kill this bitch."

"That's all I needed to hear, I'll be in touch." Jasmine walked back to her car knowing that Nikki's clock just started to wind down, Mac watched Captain Fuller from across the street as he was taking pictures of everything.

***

Mac bumped into Captain Fuller as he was walking out of the store. Captain Fuller stopped to light his cigarette when Mac walked up behind him.

"What's up, Captain… you have another one of those?" Captain Fuller looked over at Mac and handed him a cigarette.

"Where the fuck did you just come from Mac?"

"The station, I'm on my way to the house… what about you?" Captain Fuller pulled his cigarette before talking.

"I helped a few blue and whites out on a traffic stop, just some kids driving fast and racing a few blocks over. Other than that it's been a slow night, real peaceful. Enjoy your smoke, we'll talk more tomorrow… how about you come to my office, say around noon?"

"Yes sir, I'll see you then." Mac walked off from Captain Fuller knowing he just lied to his face, he couldn't trust him anymore, he was just playing both sides and the only outcome for his actions would lead up to death. Nikki was a flower that only grew in the darkness and death was the only language she knew.

***

Nikki looked at the flatbed that pulled up to her place of business with the red droptop Bentley. She was talking on the phone to Benny about the pipeline and the upcoming drop off she was about to ship down there, that's when she saw Mayhem walk up to the flatbed as he was unloading the car she just watched.

"Hey, I'm looking for Stacy Hall? I need her to sign these papers for this drop off?"

"That's not going to happen, any papers that need to be signed I'll sign them."

"I have no problem with that, I just need you to sign here, and here, and I need you to initial here, and I'll be on my way." Mayhem took the clipboard and signed off on the car, Nikki looked out the window one more time, closer to the driver of the flatbed and notice the scar on his left cheek. She had seen it before, she moved the phone from her ear and that's when it came back to her…he was one of Mrs. Blanka's assassins. He took the nightclub in Mexico by storm and killed multiple people that night by placing bombs around the club. she saw him look back at Mayhem as he got in the car. She dropped her phone and took off running to Mayhem just as she reached the shop doors she yelled.

"Mayhem, get out of the car!" Mayhem turned around and looked at Nikki but it was too late, all you heard was the sound of the explosion. Nikki was thrown back into the auto parts shop as the car was engulfed in flames. Mayhem was dead and all Nikki could do was just watch, Handrus sent her another message and one of her apes was dead now and it happened all in front of her eyes and there was nothing she could do to stop it. Nikki just looked at the car in a blaze.

Chapter 39

"Captain Fuller, yesterday Nikki was attacked by a car bomb, it killed one of her men. We have to face the facts, Captain... where there's smoke there's fire, and Nikki is under a lot of fire right now. She's in the middle of a triangle and everyone is shooting at her."

"Well, Mac... when you are the boss everyone wants you dead. Nikki is a cold-hearted killer she has more bodies on her hands than death. This is her karma coming back on her, I done seen what she's done to people. You ever hear the expression 'when the kitchen gets too hot get the fuck out of there'?"

"Yeah, I heard that before Captain."

"But you know what I do know about Nikki? When the kitchen gets too hot for everyone else it's just right for her."

"One of her men is dead, so that means a lot more people are going to die. Get ready for the blood in the streets."

"Let me tell you this, Nikki's days are coming to an end, we will be looking down at her dead body on a cold sheet of metal sooner than you think, and you can take that to the bank Mac."

"So where do we go from here Captain?"

"We watch as her empire crumbles, so we stand down."

Captain Fuller lit his cigarette.

"Yeah, get ready to watch that cold hearted bitch die."

"Sayless Captain, will that be all?"

"That will be all, things are about to get hot real soon Mac."

***

Nikki sat in her office with the doors locked, she didn't want to be bothered by nobody. Mayhem was like her son, she loved him. She was having flashbacks of all the things they did together, this one hurt her deep. She promised that death would come. She picked up her bottle of Cîroc and was drinking straight from the bottle when there was a knock at her door. She just let them knock, she wasn't in the mood for company until she heard Drama's voice "Nikki, I have Mac here. he said he needs to talk to you, that it's very important." Nikki got up and opened the door then went back to her seat and glared at both of them. They picked up on the hate and hurt in her eyes. Mac walked up to Nikki and placed the folder on her desk.

"Nikki, you have my condolences. I'm sorry about Mayhem, he was a good kid."

"Thank you Mac, I really appreciate that. So what is this you placed on my desk?"

"Pictures I took the other night of Captain Fuller with Jasmine." Nikki was looking at the pictures "Do you know what they was talking about?"

"No, but I do know he wants you dead."

"Captain Fuller is talking about having me killed is he? Mac are you sure?"

"I'm 110% sure."

Mac pulled out a tape recorder and pressed play, Nikki didn't say a word as she just listened to Captain Fuller talk about her death.

"Mac, thank you for your loyalty."

"No problem, Nikki." "Drama can you walk Mac out please?"

"Yes ma'am," Nikki knew the first thing she was going to do was kill Captain Fuller in the worst way. She was going to show him what she really was capable of doing, she told him before don't play around.

Chapter 40

Kareem woke up to Jasmine holding his hand, he opened his eyes and looked at her and with a low tone, "Jasmine, I don't know how... but he was waiting on us. He got the drop on me bad." Jasmine took her hand and rubbed his arm.

"Don't worry about that... all that matters is that you're okay, nothing else matters. I already know it was one of Nikki's guys who did this. I'm working on taking her down I just need you to rest and get better, that's all." Jasmine bent down and kissed Kareem on the forehead.

"I'll be back soon," Kareem watched as Jasmine walked out.

"Y'all three are watching him with your lives, because your lives depend on it. Do I make myself clear?"

***

Handrus stood on the deck and smoked a cigar with an all white suit on as he talked to Mecca

"So you're telling me you fucked up?"

"No boss, Nikki didn't see nobody at all. I couldn't see her, I dropped the car off and one of her top soldiers got killed with the bomb."

"Don't worry, she knows her time is coming. That was the first one signed before Santa Maria sends her death angel knocking at her door."

"So do you want me to come back to Mexico now?"

"No, stay there and keep me informed on her actions. I also need her address, because when it rains it pours."

"Yes sir," Handrus hung the phone up when his second command walked up to him.

"Carlos, I want you to take 20 plus men to New York to kill Nikki. Do not come back if she's not dead, do I make myself clear? I want everything around her dead." Carlos nodded then walked off leaving Handrus on the deck.

***

Nikki sat in the backseat of the BMW and watched as Captain Fuller left the police station, she followed him six blocks away and looked at the time on her watch. It was 8 pm Captain Fuller stopped at the red light just as Nikki's phone went off, it was Drama letting her know he was about to ram the car. Nikki cocked her gun, Captain Fuller pulled off, Drama hit the car with the SUV doing 80 mph making his car flip over. Nikki's BMW pulled over next to Captain Fuller's car, Captain Fuller was hanging out of the driver side door as people gathered around watching everything unfold, pulling their phones out and recorded everything. Then she put the murder one mask over her face as she stepped out of the car, she walked with her gun in her hand as Captain Fuller looked up at her as she pointed her gun at his face.

"I told you before, don't fuck with me... now look at you?" Captain Fuller knew that this was Nikki before he could speak. Sparks flew out of Nikki's gun as bullets were breaking through his skull. Nikki unloaded her whole clip into Captain Fuller's head. She looked at Drama as he poured gas all over the SUV sending the vehicle up in flames. He ran back to the BMW as Nikki was getting inside and they drove off, leaving Captain Fuller in a pool of blood and with people recording his body just twitching as he laid there dead.

***

"This is Barbara Wright with Channel 5 Action News with a breaking news update. As you can see behind me this is a horrible scene, we have emergency rescue teams out here along with 20 or more officers on the scene. We are witnessing our own Captain Fuller from the 26th Precinct in Brooklyn dead on the scene. We have witness statements, but before we talk to the witness, let's talk about Captain Fuller's career, he was an upstanding citizen who swore to protect and clean the streets up, today is a horrible day... Miss, what is your name?"

"My name is Kimberly West."

"Miss West, can you tell me what happened out here tonight?"

"Yes, I was standing over there at Jimmy's Pizza Parlor when I heard a big boom, that's when I saw the black BMW pull up and it looked like a female got out of the backseat and walked up to the man hanging outside the car door. I could tell she said something to him then she started shooting him point blank in the face. She watched as the other man set the black SUV on fire then she walked back to her BMW and got in, then the man ran to the BMW and got in and drove off."

"There you have it from one who witnessed the whole thing unfold. Thank you Miss West for your statement, stay tuned for more updates right here on Channel 5 Action News." Chief Ward just stared down at Captain Fuller's body and said to himself. "Captain, what did you get yourself involved with?" Chief Ward looked around the crime scene one more time at all the people walking around, he wasn't going to talk to anybody because the law of the streets means rats would eat you alive. Nobody wants to be labeled a rat, because you would be put on the grocery list.

Chapter 41

"Did you see the news?" Agent Marcus asked Director Cockright.

"Yeah I did, she's killing cops in the streets. " "You said blood in the streets, she gave you what you asked for... blood in the streets doesn't mean you can set a tree on fire and choose which way it burns. You wanted blood in the streets she's giving it to you sir." Director Cockright took his hand and rubbed his head.

"Yeah, you're right. I guess we can use this for the good, like you said she's good at what she does. One dirty cop doesn't stop what I need done, let her know I need more blood in the streets as of yesterday."

"Will do sir."

Agent Marcus got up and started to walk out of the office but stopped when Director Cockright called his name, Marcus turned around.

"Yes sir?"

"You were right, this was a win-win." Agent Marcus nodded as he walked off.

***

"Drama, I know my days are numbered so last night I made a few calls, if anything is to happen to me go to Benny with the mafia, also Agent Marcus..." Drama cut Nikki off.

"Nikki I don't want to know, because if they kill you they killed me. That's just how this shit goes." "Drama, we have a cartel to run… we have apes who died protecting the Blood Diamond Cartel because they believed in me, they believed in the cartel, and I believe in you. Everyone knows who we are, I talked to everybody last night about you, they know if anything was to happen to me that you would take my place. All contracts and agreements are bonded by blood, but if I do die… you take over as the head of the Blood Diamond Cartel." Drama shook his head but eventually agreed.

"Nikki, so where do we go from here?"

"I need you to go to Philly for a week, I have a pipeline out there and I just need you to check it out to make sure everything is good."

"When do I need to go?"

"Tonight, go get some apes to go with you."

"I will," Nikki knew the cartel was coming her way, and all she could do was prepare for the fallout. "Drama, shut the auto parts shop down as well, because a lot of motherfuckers are going to die, and we need to tie up all loose strings."

"All I ask is that I get the chance to kill the motherfucker who took my brother Mayhem from me. I want to be the one who looks in his eyes and takes his life from him."

"Just make sure you tell him I said give Mrs. Blanka my best regards from the Blood Diamond Cartel."

"I will."

"Good, now go send my shooters at Jasmine… she's at the club, we need to get that done now."

Chapter 42

"Nikki is moving reckless, she is killing cops and shooting at everyone right now. I know my name is on that grocery list, and she's trying to make a point to prove that she's not to be fucked with, but we've been doing this a lot longer, so if it isn't one of us, everyone needs the order to body them on sight. Do I make myself clear?" Jasmine looked at all her soldiers.

"Good, now is my car outside?"

"Yes, it is Jasmine. Your limo is parked out front." "Good, you two walk me outside."

Nikki had her apes outside the club just waiting for the right opportunity. The club wasn't open it was only 2:00 pm, but Jasmine was having a meeting with her guys. Jasmine was walking out the club when Nikki's apes pulled their murder one masks over their faces. Jasmine looked and saw the guns hanging out of the car window, she pulled her gun out of her Louis Vuitton bag and bit her bottom lip and yelled out.

"Y'all want to die? Let me see y'all on your fucking way, pussies." she started shooting at the car, her guys had came out and were shooting at the car as well. Bullets were flying back and forth the driver got hit in the chest, crashing the car into a parked car. Jasmine ran up to the car and was shooting inside the car, she emptied the whole clip. She looked at the driver and seen he was still alive she looked at one of her guys.

"Give me your gun now!"

he passed her his gun and she walked to the driver's side window and pointed the gun at his head.

"Nikki sent you to die pussy." she shot him point blank three times in the head. Jasmine looked around before running back into the club, she walked up to her manager.

"Delete all the video footage now before the police get down here." she looked around and walked out the back door to the club where her car was waiting on her. Within 10 minutes you had five blue and white police cars out front taping off the crime scene and asking questions.

***

Chief Ward was on the crime scene looking at how everything was unfolding, from Captain Fuller being killed last night to four dead bodies in front of Brooklyn hottest nightclub, there was a war going on in New York City and there was a lot of big players involved. That's when one of the detectives walked up to him.

"Chief, we have nothing on any of the video cameras, all of them have been erased and no one is talking."

"Yeah I know, where is the owner of this club?"

"I don't know, the manager I just spoke with said he hasn't seen her."

"Of course he hasn't. Get everything wrapped up down here and have a report on my desk as soon as possible."

"Will do, sir." Chief Ward walked to his car leaving the crime scene in a state of rage.

Chapter 43

Nikki pensively walked around her mansion, she had men everywhere… she made sure Remy stayed close to her and both of her blue pitbulls were outside as well. It wasn't quite 9 pm and she sat at her table drinking a glass of wine as she smoked her cigar, suddenly she heard a knock at the door she got up to see who was at the door, it was Remy.

"I was just coming to check on you to see if you needed anything before I turn in?"

Nikki smiled, "No beautiful, I'm okay thank you."

"Okay, I'll be downstairs if you need me."

"No, come in… let me get you something to drink."
"Okay, thank you." when Remy walked into the office Nikki closed the door behind her. Nikki's men walking around the backyard noticed one of Handrus' men edging out from behind a bush and grabbed him by the head and stabbed him in the neck killing him instantly. He laid the body down and waved for the other guys he was with to come over the gate, there were 10 of them all together.

"You five go that way, you four come with me. She has 15 men on the grounds, we don't know who has vests on, so all headshots. Once you get in the house send word so the other ten guys can come in. We are here for one job, kill Nikki… now let's go."

Remy was smiling and laughing at one of Nikki's jokes.

"Nikki that is too funny, I never saw this side of you before."

Nikki smiled sadly as she placed her drink down on the table, "no one has/"

Nikki stopped talking when she heard a gunshot, she put her hand up.

"Did you hear that?" Nikki jumped up and ran to her monitors, she looked and saw a man with mask over hia face with guns in his hands, and he wasn't the only one. She ran to her desk and pulled out both her guns and looked at Remy at the door.

"They're here, if you see any Mexicans kill them on sight. It's shoot or get shot, it's us or them remember that when you go out there." Nikki opened the door and ran to the stairs shooting two Mexicans as they tried to run up the stairs. Remy was shooting down from the stairs on the other side, all you heard was the sound of gunshots in the mansion one of Handras' men jumped on Nikki from behind, knocking her to the ground. She rolled over with her gun pointed at his chest and pulled the trigger, shooting him three times in the chest. She looked at Remy laying on the ground with her eyes open, dead as a knife was in her throat. She got up and ran to her office she closed her office door and closed her eyes taking in deep breaths, she walked to her monitors and looked at all her guys on the floor dead. Handrus' man was shooting up the dead bodies. She knew this day was coming that's why she sent Drama on a fake run to Philly so he wouldn't be there. Word got to her about Handrus' men crossing the boarder and knew they were on their way. She closed her eyes and opened them and ran to the middle of the floor downstairs and looked at all of them with both guns in her hands, she let the bullets fly hitting everything in sight. Carlos pointed the M16 at her and let the bullets rip through her body. Nikki dropped down to her knees and her guns fell out of her hands, blood was coming out of her mouth as she looked at Carlos pointing the M16 at her. "Santa Maria sent me to claim your soul." Nikki spat blood on his shoes as she grinned.

"Fuck you, *puto.*" Carlos pulled the trigger and put 20 rounds into her body as blood splattered all over the floor as her body was ripped apart. He looked at her laying on the floor in her own blood, he looked at his men that were still alive and waved to come on. Once outside they stepped over Nikki's two dead dogs, and dead bodies everywhere. His men and her men he came with 20 and was leaving with five, he pulled his phone out and called him Handrus after a few rings, Handrus picked up the phone.

"Is it done?"

"Yes, I killed her myself and told her what you said."

"Good, now come back to Mexico."

"Yes, I'm on my way now." Handrus hung up the phone knowing Nikki reign over Harlem and the Blood Diamond Cartel was over. He calmly lit his cigar knowing that Nikki's blood was now on his hands.

***

Drama pulled up to the house and saw all the red and blue flashing lights out there. You had the news team out there along with people standing around. He stepped out of the car and walked into the front yard under the caution tape right up to the house. Drama walked past 20 plus officers to the middle of the floor, he looked down at Nikki's dead body and closed his eyes as a tear fell from his eye. Officer Mac walked up to him.

"Drana, you shouldn't be here right now... you don't need to be seen here like this."

"Why? They ripped my fucking heart out of my chest, look at her... they killed my queen."

"Drama, Nikki reached out to all of us already, we all spoke a few days ago, but right now you need to leave." Drama looked at him and then Nikki one more time and walked off. Chief Ward was walking around looking at everything and all of the dead bodies as he saw Drama leaving.

Chapter 44

3 Months Later

"Jasmine, Nikki's dead, her crew is dead, we have the streets on lockdown... New York is ours again, there's no stopping us." Jasmine smiled as she looked at Kareem.

"Nikki is dead and still we stand, just because she's dead doesn't mean the war is over. There's always somebody to go to war with, there's always somebody to have beef with. I'll be back, I have a 10 pm meeting with some very important people and I don't want to be late."

"Okay, I'll see you when you get back," Jasmine walked up to the driver of the car as he opened the door for her to get inside. She waved to Kareem, Jasmine pulled out her phone and was talking as she was headed to the meeting. The car stopped at a red light and she noticed a van pulling up next to the car. The driver of the van nodded at the driver, Jasmine saw it all unfolding as she watched the van door slide open with the man holding an AR-15 letting off rounds into the backseat of the car hitting Jasmine with multiple shots. The man opened the back door to the car and looked at the dead body and fired more rounds into the car as an overkill. The driver got into the van as they pulled off, "Yo, Drama... that shit was wild!" Drama smiled as he took off his fake beard and mustache, and wig as he looked at Sid.

"One thing Nikki told me, it's not what you know... but who you know and that's a fact." he said as the van took off leaving Jasmine dead in the backseat of the car.

Two Weeks Earlier

Benny was talking to Jasmine over the phone sitting in his office as he looked at the newspaper.

"Yes, Nikki is dead and we do need a new distro for New York City Jasmine. I will be in New York in 2 weeks I will have my personal driver pick you up and bring you to my location, he will come get you from the address that you provided for me and he will be there at 10 pm sharp. I'll call you when he's out front okay?" Benny hung up the phone and look at Drama, "My part is done, make sure you do yours. I'll call you when it's time to go, just be ready and remember nothing changes with our agreement with the Blood Diamond Cartel, understood?"

"Understood." Drama turned and walked out of the office knowing that Nikki wasn't about to die alone, in Nikki's words, it's always either shoot or get shot period.

Lock Down Publications and Ca$h Presents
Assisted Publishing Packages

BASIC PACKAGE	UPGRADED PACKAGE
$499	$800
Editing	Typing
Cover Design	Editing
Formatting	Cover Design
	Formatting
ADVANCE PACKAGE	**LDP SUPREME PACKAGE**
$1,200	$1,500
Typing	Typing
Editing	Editing
Cover Design	Cover Design
Formatting	Formatting
Copyright registration	Copyright registration
Proofreading	Proofreading
Upload book to Amazon	Set up Amazon account
	Upload book to Amazon
	Advertise on LDP, Amazon and Facebook Page

***Other services available upon request.
Additional charges may apply

Lock Down Publications
P.O. Box 944
Stockbridge, GA 30281-9998
Phone: 470 303-9761

Submission Guideline

Submit the first three chapters of your completed manuscript to ldpsubmissions@gmail.com. In the subject line add **Your Book's Title**. The manuscript must be in a Word Doc file and sent as an attachment. Document should be in Times New Roman, double spaced, and in size 12 font. Also, provide your synopsis and full contact information. If sending multiple submissions, they must each be in a separate email.

Have a story but no way to send it electronically? You can still submit to LDP/Ca$h Presents. Send in the first three chapters, written or typed, of your completed manuscript to:

LDP: Submissions Dept
P.O. Box 944
Stockbridge, GA 30281-9998

DO NOT send original manuscript. Must be a duplicate. Provide your synopsis and a cover letter containing your full contact information.

Thanks for considering LDP and Ca$h Presents.

NEW RELEASES

BLOODLINE OF A SAVAGE **BY PRINCE A. TAUHID**

THE MURDER QUEENS 4 **BY MICHAEL GALLON**

THE BUTTERFLY MAFIA **BY FUMIYA PAYNE**

KING KILLA 2 **BY VINCENT "VITTO" HOLLOWAY**

BABY, I'M WINTERTIME COLD 3 **BY MEESHA**

THESE VICIOUS STREETS **BY PRINCE A. TAUHID**

TIL DEATH 2 **BY ARYANNA**

CITY OF SMOKE 2 **BY MOLOTTI**

STEPPERS **BY KING RIO**

THE LANE **BY KEN-KEN SPENCE**

MONEY GAME 2 **BY SMOOVE DOLLA**

THE BLACK DIAMOND CARTEL **BY SAYNOMORE**

CRIME BOSS 2 **BY PLAYA RAY**

THUG OF SPADES **BY COREY ROBINSON**

LOVE IN THE TRENCHES 2 **BY COREY ROBINSON**

TIL DEATH 3 **BY ARYANNA**

THE BIRTH OF A GANGSTER 4 **BY DELMONT PLAYER**

PRODUCT OF THE STREETS **BY DEMOND "MONEY" ANDERSON**

Coming Soon from Lock Down Publications/Ca$h Presents

BLOOD OF A BOSS VI
SHADOWS OF THE GAME II
TRAP BASTARD II
By **Askari**

LOYAL TO THE GAME IV
By **T.J. & Jelissa**

TRUE SAVAGE VIII
MIDNIGHT CARTEL IV
DOPE BOY MAGIC IV
CITY OF KINGZ III
NIGHTMARE ON SILENT AVE II
THE PLUG OF LIL MEXICO II
CLASSIC CITY II
By **Chris Green**

BLAST FOR ME III
A SAVAGE DOPEBOY III
CUTTHROAT MAFIA III
DUFFLE BAG CARTEL VII
HEARTLESS GOON VI
By **Ghost**

A HUSTLER'S DECEIT III
KILL ZONE II
BAE BELONGS TO ME III
TIL DEATH II
By **Aryanna**

KING OF THE TRAP III
By **T.J. Edwards**

GORILLAZ IN THE BAY V
3X KRAZY III
STRAIGHT BEAST MODE III
By **De'Kari**

KINGPIN KILLAZ IV
STREET KINGS III
PAID IN BLOOD III
CARTEL KILLAZ IV
DOPE GODS III
By **Hood Rich**

SINS OF A HUSTLA II
By **ASAD**

YAYO V
BRED IN THE GAME 2
By **S. Allen**

THE STREETS WILL TALK II
By **Yolanda Moore**

SON OF A DOPE FIEND III
HEAVEN GOT A GHETTO III
SKI MASK MONEY III
By **Renta**

LOYALTY AIN'T PROMISED III
By **Keith Williams**

I'M NOTHING WITHOUT HIS LOVE II
SINS OF A THUG II
TO THE THUG I LOVED BEFORE II
IN A HUSTLER I TRUST II
By **Monet Dragun**

QUIET MONEY IV
EXTENDED CLIP III
THUG LIFE IV
By **Trai'Quan**

THE STREETS MADE ME IV
By **Larry D. Wright**

IF YOU CROSS ME ONCE III
ANGEL V
By **Anthony Fields**

THE STREETS WILL NEVER CLOSE IV
By **K'ajji**

HARD AND RUTHLESS III
KILLA KOUNTY IV
By **Khufu**

MONEY GAME III
By **Smoove Dolla**

MURDA WAS THE CASE III
Elijah R. Freeman

AN UNFORESEEN LOVE IV
BABY, I'M WINTERTIME COLD III
By **Meesha**

QUEEN OF THE ZOO III
By **Black Migo**

CONFESSIONS OF A JACKBOY III
By **Nicholas Lock**

JACK BOYS VS DOPE BOYS IV
A GANGSTA'S QUR'AN V
COKE GIRLZ II
COKE BOYS II
LIFE OF A SAVAGE V
CHI'RAQ GANGSTAS V
SOSA GANG III
BRONX SAVAGES II
BODYMORE KINGPINS II
By **Romell Tukes**

KING KILLA II
By **Vincent "Vitto" Holloway**

BETRAYAL OF A THUG III
By **Fre$h**

THE MURDER QUEENS III
By **Michael Gallon**

THE BIRTH OF A GANGSTER III
By **Delmont Player**

TREAL LOVE II
By **Le'Monica Jackson**

FOR THE LOVE OF BLOOD III
By **Jamel Mitchell**

RAN OFF ON DA PLUG II
By **Paper Boi Rari**

HOOD CONSIGLIERE III
By **Keese**

PRETTY GIRLS DO NASTY THINGS II
By **Nicole Goosby**

PROTÉGÉ OF A LEGEND III
LOVE IN THE TRENCHES II
By **Corey Robinson**

IT'S JUST ME AND YOU II
By **Ah'Million**

FOREVER GANGSTA III
By **Adrian Dulan**

GORILLAZ IN THE TRENCHES II
By **SayNoMore**

THE COCAINE PRINCESS VIII
By **King Rio**

CRIME BOSS II
By **Playa Ray**

LOYALTY IS EVERYTHING III
By **Molotti**

HERE TODAY GONE TOMORROW II
By **Fly Rock**

REAL G'S MOVE IN SILENCE II
By **Von Diesel**

GRIMEY WAYS IV
By **Ray Vinci**

Available Now

RESTRAINING ORDER I & II
By **CA$H & Coffee**

LOVE KNOWS NO BOUNDARIES I II & III
By **Coffee**

RAISED AS A GOON I, II, III & IV
BRED BY THE SLUMS I, II, III
BLAST FOR ME I & II
ROTTEN TO THE CORE I II III
A BRONX TALE I, II, III
DUFFLE BAG CARTEL I II III IV V VI
HEARTLESS GOON I II III IV V
A SAVAGE DOPEBOY I II
DRUG LORDS I II III
CUTTHROAT MAFIA I II
KING OF THE TRENCHES
By **Ghost**

LAY IT DOWN I & II
LAST OF A DYING BREED I II
BLOOD STAINS OF A SHOTTA I & II III
By **Jamaica**

LOYAL TO THE GAME I II III
LIFE OF SIN I, II III
By **TJ & Jelissa**

IF LOVING HIM IS WRONG…I & II
LOVE ME EVEN WHEN IT HURTS I II III
By **Jelissa**

BLOODY COMMAS I & II
SKI MASK CARTEL I, II & III
KING OF NEW YORK I II, III IV V
RISE TO POWER I II III
COKE KINGS I II III IV V
BORN HEARTLESS I II III IV
KING OF THE TRAP I II
By **T.J. Edwards**

WHEN THE STREETS CLAP BACK I & II III
THE HEART OF A SAVAGE I II III IV
MONEY MAFIA I II
LOYAL TO THE SOIL I II III
By **Jibril Williams**

A DISTINGUISHED THUG STOLE MY HEART I II &
III
LOVE SHOULDN'T HURT I II III IV
RENEGADE BOYS I II III IV
PAID IN KARMA I II III
SAVAGE STORMS I II III
AN UNFORESEEN LOVE I II III
BABY, I'M WINTERTIME COLD I II
By **Meesha**

A GANGSTER'S CODE I &, II III
A GANGSTER'S SYN I II III
THE SAVAGE LIFE I II III
CHAINED TO THE STREETS I II III
BLOOD ON THE MONEY I II III
A GANGSTA'S PAIN I II III
By **J-Blunt**

PUSH IT TO THE LIMIT
By **Bre' Hayes**

BLOOD OF A BOSS I, II, III, IV, V
SHADOWS OF THE GAME
TRAP BASTARD
By **Askari**

THE STREETS BLEED MURDER I, II & III
THE HEART OF A GANGSTA I II& III
By **Jerry Jackson**

CUM FOR ME I II III IV V VI VII VIII
An **LDP Erotica Collaboration**

BRIDE OF A HUSTLA I II & II
THE FETTI GIRLS I, II& III
CORRUPTED BY A GANGSTA I, II III, IV
BLINDED BY HIS LOVE
THE PRICE YOU PAY FOR LOVE I, II ,III
DOPE GIRL MAGIC I II III
By **Destiny Skai**

WHEN A GOOD GIRL GOES BAD
By **Adrienne**

A GANGSTER'S REVENGE I II III & IV
THE BOSS MAN'S DAUGHTERS I II III IV V
A SAVAGE LOVE I & II
BAE BELONGS TO ME I II
A HUSTLER'S DECEIT I, II, III
WHAT BAD BITCHES DO I, II, III
SOUL OF A MONSTER I II III
KILL ZONE
A DOPE BOY'S QUEEN I II III
TIL DEATH
By **Aryanna**

THE COST OF LOYALTY I II III
By Kweli

A KINGPIN'S AMBITION
A KINGPIN'S AMBITION **II**
I MURDER FOR THE DOUGH
By **Ambitious**

TRUE SAVAGE I II III IV V VI VII
DOPE BOY MAGIC I, II, III
MIDNIGHT CARTEL I II III
CITY OF KINGZ I II
NIGHTMARE ON SILENT AVE
THE PLUG OF LIL MEXICO II
CLASSIC CITY
By **Chris Green**

A DOPEBOY'S PRAYER
By **Eddie "Wolf" Lee**

THE KING CARTEL I, II & III
By **Frank Gresham**

THESE NIGGAS AIN'T LOYAL I, II & III
By **Nikki Tee**

GANGSTA SHYT I II &III
By **CATO**

THE ULTIMATE BETRAYAL
By **Phoenix**

BOSS'N UP I, II & III
By **Royal Nicole**

I LOVE YOU TO DEATH
By **Destiny J**

I RIDE FOR MY HITTA
I STILL RIDE FOR MY HITTA
By **Misty Holt**

LOVE & CHASIN' PAPER
By **Qay Crockett**

TO DIE IN VAIN
SINS OF A HUSTLA
By **ASAD**

BROOKLYN HUSTLAZ
By **Boogsy Morina**

BROOKLYN ON LOCK I & II
By **Sonovia**

GANGSTA CITY
By **Teddy Duke**

A DRUG KING AND HIS DIAMOND I & II III
A DOPEMAN'S RICHES
HER MAN, MINE'S TOO I, II
CASH MONEY HO'S
THE WIFEY I USED TO BE I II
PRETTY GIRLS DO NASTY THINGS
By Nicole Goosby

LIPSTICK KILLAH I, II, III
CRIME OF PASSION I II & III
FRIEND OR FOE I II III
By **Mimi**

TRAPHOUSE KING I II & III
KINGPIN KILLAZ I II III
STREET KINGS I II
PAID IN BLOOD I II
CARTEL KILLAZ I II III
DOPE GODS I II
By **Hood Rich**

STEADY MOBBN' I, II, III
THE STREETS STAINED MY SOUL I II III
By **Marcellus Allen**

WHO SHOT YA I, II, III
SON OF A DOPE FIEND I II
HEAVEN GOT A GHETTO I II
SKI MASK MONEY I II
By **Renta**

GORILLAZ IN THE BAY I II III IV
TEARS OF A GANGSTA I II
3X KRAZY I II
STRAIGHT BEAST MODE I II
By **DE'KARI**

TRIGGADALE I II III
MURDA WAS THE CASE I II
By **Elijah R. Freeman**

THE STREETS ARE CALLING
By **Duquie Wilson**

SLAUGHTER GANG I II III
RUTHLESS HEART I II III
By **Willie Slaughter**

GOD BLESS THE TRAPPERS I, II, III
THESE SCANDALOUS STREETS I, II, III
FEAR MY GANGSTA I, II, III IV, V
THESE STREETS DON'T LOVE NOBODY I, II
BURY ME A G I, II, III, IV, V
A GANGSTA'S EMPIRE I, II, III, IV
THE DOPEMAN'S BODYGAURD I II
THE REALEST KILLAZ I II III
THE LAST OF THE OGS I II III
By **Tranay Adams**

MARRIED TO A BOSS I II III
By **Destiny Skai & Chris Green**

KINGZ OF THE GAME I II III IV V VI VII
CRIME BOSS
By **Playa Ray**

FUK SHYT
By **Blakk Diamond**

DON'T F#CK WITH MY HEART I II
By **Linnea**

ADDICTED TO THE DRAMA I II III
IN THE ARM OF HIS BOSS II
By **Jamila**

YAYO I II III IV
A SHOOTER'S AMBITION I II
BRED IN THE GAME
By **S. Allen**

LOYALTY AIN'T PROMISED I II
By **Keith Williams**

TRAP GOD I II III
RICH $AVAGE I II III
MONEY IN THE GRAVE I II III
By **Martell Troublesome Bolden**

FOREVER GANGSTA I II
GLOCKS ON SATIN SHEETS I II
By **Adrian Dulan**

TOE TAGZ I II III IV
LEVELS TO THIS SHYT I II
IT'S JUST ME AND YOU
By **Ah'Million**

KINGPIN DREAMS I II III
RAN OFF ON DA PLUG
By **Paper Boi Rari**

CONFESSIONS OF A GANGSTA I II III IV
CONFESSIONS OF A JACKBOY I II
By **Nicholas Lock**

I'M NOTHING WITHOUT HIS LOVE
SINS OF A THUG
TO THE THUG I LOVED BEFORE
A GANGSTA SAVED XMAS
IN A HUSTLER I TRUST
By **Monet Dragun**

QUIET MONEY I II III
THUG LIFE I II III
EXTENDED CLIP I II
A GANGSTA'S PARADISE
By **Trai'Quan**

CAUGHT UP IN THE LIFE I II III
THE STREETS NEVER LET GO I II III
By **Robert Baptiste**

NEW TO THE GAME I II III
MONEY, MURDER & MEMORIES I II III
By **Malik D. Rice**

CREAM I II III
THE STREETS WILL TALK
By **Yolanda Moore**

LIFE OF A SAVAGE I II III IV
A GANGSTA'S QUR'AN I II III IV
MURDA SEASON I II III
GANGLAND CARTEL I II III
CHI'RAQ GANGSTAS I II III IV
KILLERS ON ELM STREET I II III
JACK BOYZ N DA BRONX I II III
A DOPEBOY'S DREAM I II III
JACK BOYS VS DOPE BOYS I II III
COKE GIRLZ
COKE BOYS
SOSA GANG I II
BRONX SAVAGES
BODYMORE KINGPINS
By **Romell Tukes**

THE STREETS MADE ME I II III
By **Larry D. Wright**

CONCRETE KILLA I II III
VICIOUS LOYALTY I II III
By **Kingpen**

THE ULTIMATE SACRIFICE I, II, III, IV, V, VI
KHADIFI
IF YOU CROSS ME ONCE I II
ANGEL I II III IV
IN THE BLINK OF AN EYE
By **Anthony Fields**

THE LIFE OF A HOOD STAR
By **Ca$h & Rashia Wilson**

THE STREETS WILL NEVER CLOSE I II III
By **K'ajji**

NIGHTMARES OF A HUSTLA I II III
By **King Dream**

HARD AND RUTHLESS I II
MOB TOWN 251
THE BILLIONAIRE BENTLEYS I II III
REAL G'S MOVE IN SILENCE
By **Von Diesel**

GHOST MOB
By **Stilloan Robinson**

MOB TIES I II III IV V VI
SOUL OF A HUSTLER, HEART OF A KILLER I II
GORILLAZ IN THE TRENCHES
By **SayNoMore**

BODYMORE MURDERLAND I II III
THE BIRTH OF A GANGSTER I II
By **Delmont Player**

FOR THE LOVE OF A BOSS
By **C. D. Blue**

KILLA KOUNTY I II III IV
By Khufu

MOBBED UP I II III IV
THE BRICK MAN I II III IV V
THE COCAINE PRINCESS I II III IV V VI VII
By **King Rio**

MONEY GAME I II
By **Smoove Dolla**

A GANGSTA'S KARMA I II III
By **FLAME**

KING OF THE TRENCHES I II III
By **GHOST & TRANAY ADAMS**

QUEEN OF THE ZOO I II
By **Black Migo**

GRIMEY WAYS I II III
By **Ray Vinci**

XMAS WITH AN ATL SHOOTER
By **Ca$h & Destiny Skai**

KING KILLA
By **Vincent "Vitto" Holloway**

BETRAYAL OF A THUG I II
By **Fre$h**

THE MURDER QUEENS I II
By **Michael Gallon**

TREAL LOVE
By **Le'Monica Jackson**

FOR THE LOVE OF BLOOD I II
By **Jamel Mitchell**

HOOD CONSIGLIERE I II
By **Keese**

PROTÉGÉ OF A LEGEND I II
LOVE IN THE TRENCHES
By **Corey Robinson**

BORN IN THE GRAVE I II III
By **Self Made Tay**

MOAN IN MY MOUTH
By **XTASY**

TORN BETWEEN A GANGSTER AND A
GENTLEMAN
By **J-BLUNT & Miss Kim**

LOYALTY IS EVERYTHING I II
By **Molotti**

HERE TODAY GONE TOMORROW
By **Fly Rock**

PILLOW PRINCESS
By **S. Hawkins**

SANCTIFIED AND HORNY
by **XTASY**

THE PLUG OF LIL MEXICO 2
by **CHRIS GREEN**

THE BLACK DIAMOND CARTEL
by **SAYNOMORE**

THE BIRTH OF A GANGSTER 3
by **DELMONT PLAYER**

BOOKS BY LDP'S CEO, CA$H

TRUST IN NO MAN
TRUST IN NO MAN 2
TRUST IN NO MAN 3
BONDED BY BLOOD
SHORTY GOT A THUG
THUGS CRY
THUGS CRY 2
THUGS CRY 3
TRUST NO BITCH
TRUST NO BITCH 2
TRUST NO BITCH 3
TIL MY CASKET DROPS
RESTRAINING ORDER
RESTRAINING ORDER 2
IN LOVE WITH A CONVICT
LIFE OF A HOOD STAR
XMAS WITH AN ATL SHOOTER